Marx Joyce Abbott Hardy Montaigne Machiavelli Chesterton Cooper Emerson Austen Defoe Melville Haggard Hugo Eliot Grimm Christie Carroll Stoker Molière Wilde Maupassant Byron Schiller Garnett Fitzgerald Einstein Engels Smith Goethe Hawthorne Kafka Cotton Dostoyevsky Hall Baum Kipling Doyle Willis Leslie Dumas Henry Nietzsche Flaubert Turgenev Balzac Stockton Vatsyayana Crane Burroughs Whitman Verne Curtis Tocqueville Gogol Vinci Homer Widger Tolstoy Busch Darwin Thoreau Potter Freud Zola Twain Plato Scott Lawrence Kant Jowett Stevenson Dickens Andersen Burton Hesse Harte London Descartes Cervantes Poe Aristotle Wells Voltaire Hale James Hastings Cooke Bunner Shakespeare Richter Chambers Irving Doré Swift Dante Chekhov da Shaw Wodehouse Benedict Alcott Pushkin Newton

tredition®

tredition was established in 2006 by Sandra Latusseck and Soenke Schulz. Based in Hamburg, Germany, tredition offers publishing solutions to authors and publishing houses, combined with worldwide distribution of printed and digital book content. tredition is uniquely positioned to enable authors and publishing houses to create books on their own terms and without conventional manufacturing risks.

For more information please visit: www.tredition.com

TREDITION CLASSICS

This book is part of the TREDITION CLASSICS series. The creators of this series are united by passion for literature and driven by the intention of making all public domain books available in printed format again - worldwide. Most TREDITION CLASSICS titles have been out of print and off the bookstore shelves for decades. At tredition we believe that a great book never goes out of style and that its value is eternal. Several mostly non-profit literature projects provide content to tredition. To support their good work, tredition donates a portion of the proceeds from each sold copy. As a reader of a TREDITION CLASSICS book, you support our mission to save many of the amazing works of world literature from oblivion. See all available books at www.tredition.com.

Project Gutenberg

The content for this book has been graciously provided by Project Gutenberg. Project Gutenberg is a non-profit organization founded by Michael Hart in 1971 at the University of Illinois. The mission of Project Gutenberg is simple: To encourage the creation and distribution of eBooks. Project Gutenberg is the first and largest collection of public domain eBooks.

Beaumont & Fletcher's Works

(1 of 10) - the Custom of the Country

Francis Beaumont

Imprint

This book is part of TREDITION CLASSICS

Author: Francis Beaumont
Cover design: Buchgut, Berlin – Germany

Publisher: tredition GmbH, Hamburg - Germany
ISBN: 978-3-8424-4433-1

www.tredition.com
www.tredition.de

The intention of the TREDITION CLASSICS series is to make world literature in the public domain available in printed format. Literary enthusiasts and organizations, such as Project Gutenberg, worldwide have scanned and digitally edited the original texts. tredition has subsequently formatted and redesigned the content into a modern reading layout. Therefore, we cannot guarantee the exact reproduction of the original format of a particular historic edition. Please also note that no modifications have been made to the spelling, therefore it may differ from the orthography used today.

THE CUSTOM OF THE COUNTRY.

* * * * *

Persons Represented in the Play.

Count Clodio, *Governour and a dishonourable pursuer of* Zenocia.
Manuel du Sosa, *Governour of* Lisbon, *and Brother to* Guiomar.
Arnoldo, *A Gentleman contracted to* Zenocia.
Rutilio, *A merry Gentleman Brother to* Arnoldo.
Charino, *Father to* Zenocia.
Duarte, *Son to* Guiomar, *a Gentleman well qualified but vain glorious.*
Alonzo, *a young* Portugal *Gentleman, enemy to* Duarte.
Leopold, *a Sea Captain Enamour'd on* Hippolyta.
Zabulon, *a* Jew, *servant to* Hippolyta.
Jaques, *servant to* Sulpitia.
Doctor.
Chirurgion.
Officers.
Guard.
Page.
Bravo.
Knaves, *of the Male Stewes.*
Servants.

WOMEN.

Zenocia, *Mistress to* Arnoldo, *and a chaste Wife.*
Guiomar, *a vertuous Lady, Mother to* Duarte.
Hippolyta, *a rich Lady, wantonly in Love with* Arnoldo.
Sulpitia, *a Bawd, Mistress of the Male Stewes.*

* * * * *

The Scene sometimes Lisbon, *sometimes* Italy.

* * * * *

The principal Actors were *Joseph Taylor. Robert Benfeild. John Lowin. William Eglestone. Nicholas Toolie. Richard Sharpe. John Underwood. Thomas Holcomb.*

* * * * *

Actus primus. Scena prima.

Enter Rutilio, *and* Arnold[o].

Rut. Why do you grieve thus still?

Arn. 'Twould melt a Marble, And tame a Savage man, to feel my fortune.

Rut. What fortune? I have liv'd this thirty years,
And run through all these follies you call fortunes,
Yet never fixt on any good and constant,
But what I made myself: why should I grieve then
At that I may mould any way?

Arn. You are wide still.

Rut. You love a Gentlewoman, a young handsom woman, I have lov'd a thosand, not so few.

Arn. You are dispos'd.

Rut. You hope to Marry her; 'tis a lawful calling
And prettily esteem'd of, but take heed then,
Take heed dear Brother of a stranger fortune
Than e're you felt yet; fortune my foe is a friend to it.

Arn. 'Tis true I love, dearly, and truly love, A noble, vertuous, and most beauteous Maid, And am belov'd again.

Rut. That's too much o' Conscience, To love all these would run me out o' my wits.

Arn. Prethee give ear, I am to Marry her.

Rut. Dispatch it then, and I'le go call the Piper.

Arn. But O the wicked Custom of this Country, The barbarous, most inhumane, damned Custom.

Rut. 'Tis true, to marry is a Custom
I' the world; for look you Brother,
Wou'd any man stand plucking for the Ace of Harts,
With one pack of Cards all dayes on's life?

Arn. You do not Or else you purpose not to understand me.

Rut. Proceed, I will give ear.

Arn. They have a Custom In this most beastly Country, out upon't.

Rut. Let's hear it first.

Arn. That when a Maid is contracted
And ready for the tye o'th' Church, the Governour,
He that commands in chief, must have her Maiden-head,
Or Ransom it for mony at his pleasure.

Rut. How might a man atchieve that place? a rare Custom! An admirable rare Custom: and none excepted?

Arn. None, none.

Rut. The rarer still: how could I lay about me, In this rare Office? are they born to it, or chosen?

Arn. Both equal damnable.

Rut. Me thinks both excellent, Would I were the next heir.

Arn. To this mad fortune Am I now come, my Marriage is proclaim'd, And nothing can redeem me from this mischief.

Rut. She's very young.

Arn. Yes.

Rut. And fair I dare proclaim her, Else mine eyes fail.

Arn. Fair as the bud unblasted.

Rut. I cannot blame him then, if 'twere mine own case, I would not go an Ace less.

Arn. Fye *Rutilio*, Why do you make your brothers misery Your sport and game?

Rut. There is no pastime like it.

Arn. I look'd for your advice, your timely Counsel, How to avoid this blow, not to be mockt at, And my afflictions jeer'd.

Rut. I tell thee *Arnoldo,*
An thou wert my Father, as thou art but my Brother,
My younger Brother too, I must be merry.
And where there is a wench yet can, a young wench,
A handsome wench, and sooner a good turn too,
An I were to be hang'd, thus must I handle it.
But you shall see Sir, I can change this habit
To do you any service; advise what you please,
And see with what Devotion I'le attend it?
But yet me thinks, I am taken with this Custom,

[*Enter* Charino *and* Zenocia.

And could pretend to th' place.

Arn. Draw off a little; Here comes my Mistress and her Father.

Rut. A dainty wench! Wou'd I might farm his Custom.

Char. My dear Daughter,
Now to bethink your self of new advice
Will be too late, later this timeless sorrow,
No price, nor prayers, can infringe the fate
Your beauty hath cast on yo[u], my best *Zenocia,*
Be rul'd by me, a Fathers care directs ye,
Look on the Count, look chearfully and sweetly;
What though he have the power to possess ye,
To pluck your Maiden honour, and then slight ye
By Custom unresistible to enjoy you;
Yet my sweet Child, so much your youth and goodness,
The beauty of your soul, and Saint-like Modesty,
Have won upon his mild mind, so much charm'd him,
That all power laid aside, what Law allows him,
Or sudden fires, kindled from those bright eyes,
He sues to be your servant, fairly, nobly
For ever to be tyed your faithful Husband:

Consider my best child.

Zeno. I have considered.

Char. The blessedness that this breeds too, consider
Besides your Fathers Honour, your own peace,
The banishment for ever of this Custom,
This base and barbarous use, for after once
He has found the happiness of holy Marriage,
And what it is to grow up with one Beauty,
How he will scorn and kick at such an heritage
Left him by lust and lewd progenitors.
All Virgins too, shall bless your name, shall Saint it,
And like so many Pilgrims go to your shrine,
When time has turn'd your beauty into ashes,
Fill'd with your pious memory.

Zeno. Good Father Hide not that bitter Pill I loath to swallow In such sweet words.

Char. The Count's a handsome Gentleman,
And having him, y'are certain of a fortune,
A high and noble fortune to attend you:
Where if you fling your Love upon this stranger
This young *Arnoldo,* not knowing from what place
Or honourable strain of blood he is sprung, you venture
All your own sweets, and my long cares to nothing,
Nor are you certain of his faith; why may not that
Wander as he does, every where?

Zen. No more Sir;
I must not hear, I dare not hear him wrong'd thus,
Vertue is never wounded, but I suffer.
'Tis an ill Office in your age, a poor one,
To judge thus weakly: and believe your self too,
A weaker, to betray your innocent Daughter,
To his intemp'rate, rude, and wild embraces,

She hates as Heaven hates falshood.

Rut. A good wench, She sticks close to you Sir.

Zeno. His faith uncertain?
The nobleness his vertue springs from, doubted?
D'ye doubt it is day now? or when your body's perfect,
Your stomach's well dispos'd, your pulse's temperate,
D'ye doubt you are in health? I tell you Father,
One hour of this mans goodness, this mans Nobleness
Put in the Scale, against the Counts whole being,
Forgive his lusts too, which are half his life,
He could no more endure to hold weight with him;
Arnoldo's very looks, are fair examples;
His common and indifferent actions,
Rules and strong ties of vertue: he has my first love,
To him in sacred vow I have given this body,
In him my mind inhabits.

Rut. Good wench still.

Zeno. And till he fling me off, as undeserving, Which I confess I am, of such a blessing, But would be loth to find it so—

Arn. O never;
Never my happy Mistress, never, never,
When your poor servant lives but in your favour,
One foot i'th' grave the other shall not linger.
What sacrifice of thanks, what age of service,
What danger, of more dreadful look than death,
What willing Martyrdom to crown me constant
May merit such a goodness, such a sweetness?
A love so Nobly great, no power can ruine;
Most blessed Maid go on, the Gods that gave this,
This pure unspotted love, the Child of Heaven,
In their own goodness, must preserve and save it,
And raise you a reward beyond our recompence.

Zeno. I ask but you, a pure Maid to possess, And then they have crown'd my wishes: If I fall then Go seek some better love, mine will debase you.

Rut. A pretty innocent fool; well, Governour,
Though I think well of your custom, and could wish my self
For this night in your place, heartily wish it:
Yet if you play not fair play and above board too,
I have a foolish gin here, I say no more;
I'le tell you what, and if your honours guts are not inchanted.

Arn. I should now chide you Sir, for so declining
The goodness and the grace you have ever shew'd me,
And your own vertue too, in seeking rashly
To violate that love Heaven has appointed,
To wrest your Daughters thoughts, part that affection
That both our hearts have tyed, and seek to give it.

Rut. To a wild fellow, that would weary her;
A Cannibal, that feeds on the heads of Maids,
Then flings their bones and bodies to the Devil,
Would any man of discretion venture such a gristle,
To the rude clawes of such a *Cat-a-mountain*?
You had better tear her between two Oaks, a Town Bull
Is a meer *Stoick* to this fellow, a grave Philosopher,
And a *Spanish* Jennet, a most vertuous Gentleman.

Arn. Does this seem handsome Sir?

Rut. Though I confess
Any man would desire to have her, and by any means,
At any rate too, yet that this common Hangman,
That hath whipt off the heads of a thousand maids already,
That he should glean the Harvest, sticks in my stomach:
This Rogue breaks young wenches to the Saddle,
And teaches them to stumble ever after;
That he should have her? for my Brother now
That is a handsome young fellow; and well thought on,

And will deal tenderly in the business;
Or for my self that have a reputation,
And have studied the conclusions of these causes,
And know the perfect manage, I'le tell you old Sir,
If I should call you wise Sir, I should bely you,
This thing, you study to betray your child to,
This Maiden-monger. When you have done your best,
And think you have fixt her in the point of honour,
Who do you think you have tyed her to? a Surgeon,
I must confess an excellent dissector,
One that has cut up more young tender Lamb-pies—

Char. What I spake Gentlemen, was meer compulsion,
No Fathers free-will, nor did I touch your person
With any edge of spight; or strain your loves
With any base, or hir'd perswasions;
Witness these tears, how well I wisht your fortunes. [*Exit.*

Rut. There's some grace in thee yet, you are determined To marry this Count, Lady.

Zen. Marry him *Rutilio*?

Rut. Marry him, and lye with him I mean.

Zen. You cannot mean that,
If you be a true Gentleman, you dare not,
The Brother to this man, and one that loves him;
I'le marry the Devil first.

Rut. A better choice And lay his horns by, a handsomer bed-fellow, A cooler o' my conscience.

Arn. Pray let me ask you;
And my dear Mistris, be not angry with me
For what I shall propound, I am confident,
No promise, nor no power, can force your love,
I mean in way of marriage, never stir you,
Nor to forget my faith, no state can wound you.
But for this Custom, which this wretched country

Hath wrought into a law, and must be satisfied;
Where all the pleas of honour are but laught at,
And modesty regarded as a may-game,
What shall be here considered? power we have none,
To make resistance, nor policie to cross it:
'Tis held Religion too, to pay this duty.

Zeno. I'le dye an *Atheist* then.

Arn. My noblest Mistris,
Not that I wish it so, but say it were so,
Say you did render up part of your honour,
For whilst your will is clear, all cannot perish;
Say for one night you entertain'd this monster,
Should I esteem you worse, forc'd to this render?
Your mind I know is pure, and full as beauteous;
After this short eclipse, you would rise again,
And shaking off that cloud, spread all your lustre.

Zeno. Who made you witty, to undoe your self, Sir?
Or are you loaden, with the love I bring you,
And fain would fling that burthen on another?
Am I grown common in your eyes *Arnoldo*?
Old, or unworthy of your fellowship?
D'ye think because a woman, I must err,
And therefore rather wish that fall before-hand
Coloured with Custom, not to be resisted?
D'ye love as painters doe, only some pieces,
Some certain handsome touches of your Mistris,
And let the mind pass by you, unexamined?
Be not abus'd; with what the maiden vessel
Is seasoned first, you understand the proverb.

Rut. I am afraid, this thing will make me vertuous.

Zeno. Should you lay by the least part of that love
Y'ave sworn is mine, your youth and faith has given me,
To entertain another, nay a fairer,

And make the case thus desp'rate, she must dy else;
D'ye think I would give way, or count this honest?
Be not deceiv'd, these eyes should never see you more,
This tongue forget to name you, and this heart
Hate you, as if you were born, my full *Antipathie*.
Empire and more imperious love, alone
Rule, and admit no rivals: the purest springs
When they are courted by lascivious land-floods,
Their maiden pureness, and their coolness perish.
And though they purge again to their first beauty,
The sweetness of their taste is clean departed.
I must have all or none; and am not worthy
Longer the noble name of wife, *Arnoldo*,
Than I can bring a whole heart pure and handsom.

Arnol. I never shall deserve you: not to thank you;
You are so heavenly good, no man can reach you:
I am sorrie I spake so rashly, 'twas but to try you.

Rut. You might have tryed a thousand women so, And 900, fourscore and 19 should ha' followed your counsel. Take heed o' clapping spurrs to such free cattell.

Arn. We must bethink us suddenly and constantly, And wisely too, we expect no common danger.

Zen. Be most assur'd, I'le dye first.

Enter Clodio, *and* Guard.

Rut. An't come to that once,
The Devil pick his bones, that dyes a coward,
I'le jog along with you, here comes the Stallion,
How smug he looks upon the imagination
Of what he hopes to act! pox on your kidneys;
How they begin to melt! how big he bears,
Sure he will leap before us all: what a sweet company
Of rogues and panders wait upon his lewdness!
Plague of your chops, you ha' more handsome bitts,
Than a hundred honester men, and more deserving.

How the dogg leers.

Clod. You need not now be jealous, I speak at distance to your wife, but when the Priest has done, We shall grow nearer, and more familiar.

Rut. I'le watch you for that trick, baboon, I'le
Smoke you: the rogue sweats, as if he had eaten
Grains, he broyles, if I do come to the
Basting of you.

Arno. Your Lordship
May happily speak this, to fright a stranger,
But 'tis not in your honour, to perform it;
The Custom of this place, if such there be,
At best most damnable, may urge you to it,
But if you be an honest man you hate it,
How ever I will presently prepare
To make her mine, and most undoubtedly
Believe you are abus'd, this custome feign'd too,
And what you now pretend, most fair and vertuous.

Clod. Go and believe, a good belief does well Sir; And you Sir, clear the place, but leave her here.

Arn. Your Lordships pleasure.

Clod. That anon *Arnoldo*, This is but talk.

Rut. Shall we goe off?

Arn. By any means,
I know she has pious thoughts enough to guard her:
Besides, here's nothing due to him till the tye be done,
Nor dare he offer.

Rut. Now do I long to worry him: Pray have a care to the main chance.

Zen. Pray Sir, fear not. [*Exit* Ar. *and* Rut.

Clod. Now, what say you to me?

Zen. Sir it becomes The modestie, that maids are ever born with, To use few words.

Clod. Do you see nothing in me?
Nothing to catch your eyes, nothing of wonder
The common mould of men, come short, and want in?
Do you read no future fortune for your self here?
And what a happiness it may be to you,
To have him honour you, all women aim at?
To have him love you Lady, that man love you,
The best, and the most beauteous have run mad for?
Look and be wise, you have a favour offer'd you
I do not every day propound to women;
You are a prettie one; and though each hour
I am glutted with the sacrifice of beautie,
I may be brought, as you may handle it,
To cast so good a grace and liking on you.
You understand, come kiss me, and be joyfull,
I give you leave.

Zen. Faith Sir, 'twill not shew handsome; Our sex is blushing, full of fear, unskil'd too In these alarms.

Clod. Learn then and be perfect.

Zen. I do beseech your honour pardon me, And take some skilfull one can hold you play, I am a fool.

Clod. I tell thee maid I love thee,
Let that word make thee happie, so far love thee,
That though I may enjoy thee without ceremony,
I will descend so low, to marry thee,
Me thinks I see the race that shall spring from us,
Some Princes, some great Souldiers.

Zen. I am afraid Your honour's couzen'd in this calculation; For certain, I shall ne're have a child by you.

Clod. Why?

Zen. Because I must not think to marry you, I dare not Sir, the step betwixt your honour, And my poor humble State.

Clod. I will descend to thee, And buoy thee up.

Zen. I'le sink to th' Center first.
Why would your Lordship marry, and confine that pleasure
You ever have had freely cast upon you?
Take heed my Lord, this marrying is a mad matter,
Lighter a pair of shackles will hang on you,
And quieter a quartane feaver find you.
If you wed me I must enjoy you only,
Your eyes must be called home, your thoughts in cages,
To sing to no ears then but mine; your heart bound,
The custom, that your youth was ever nurst in,
Must be forgot, I shall forget my duty else,
And how that will appear—

Clod. Wee'l talk of that more.

Zen. Besides I tell ye, I am naturally,
As all young women are, that shew like handsome,
Exceeding proud, being commended, monstrous.
Of an unquiet temper, seldom pleas'd,
Unless it be with infinite observance,
Which you were never bred to; once well angred,
As every cross in us, provokes that passion,
And like a Sea, I roule, toss, and chafe a week after.
And then all mischief I can think upon,
Abusing of your bed the least and poorest,
I tell you what you'le finde, and in these fitts,
This little beauty you are pleased to honour,
Will be so chang'd, so alter'd to an ugliness,
To such a vizard, ten to one, I dye too,
Take't then upon my death you murder'd me.

Clod. Away, away fool, why dost thou proclame these To prevent that in me, thou hast chosen in another?

Zen. Him I have chosen, I can rule and master,
Temper to what I please, you are a great one
Of a strong will to bend, I dare not venture.
Be wise my Lord, and say you were well counsel'd,
Take mony for my ransom, and forget me,
'Twill be both safe, and noble for your honour,
And wheresoever my fortunes shall conduct me,
So worthy mentions I shall render of you,
So vertuous and so fair.

Clod. You will not marrie me?

Zen. I do beseech your honour, be not angry At what I say, I cannot love ye, dare not; But set a ransom, for the flowr you covet.

Clod. No mony, nor no prayers, shall redeem that, Not all the art you have.

Zen. Set your own price Sir.

Clod. Goe to your wedding, never kneel to me,
When that's done, you are mine, I will enjoy you:
Your tears do nothing, I will not lose my custom
To cast upon my self an Empires fortune.

Zen. My mind shall not pay this custom, cruel man. [*Ex*.

Clod. Your body will content me: I'le look for you. [*Ex*.

Enter Charino, *and servants in blacks. Covering the place with blacks.*

Char. Strew all your withered flowers, your Autumn sweets
By the hot Sun ravisht of bud and beauty
Thus round about her Bride-bed, hang those blacks there
The emblemes of her honour lost; all joy
That leads a Virgin to receive her lover,
Keep from this place, all fellow-maids that bless her,
And blushing do unloose her Zone, keep from her:
No merry noise nor lusty songs be heard here,
Nor full cups crown'd with wine make the rooms giddy,
This is no masque of mirth, but murdered honour.
Sing mournfully that sad Epithalamion

I gave thee now: and prethee let thy lute weep.

Song, Dance. *Enter* Rutilio.

Rut. How now, what livery's this? do you call this a wedding? This is more like a funeral.

Char. It is one,
And my poor Daughter going to her grave,
To his most loath'd embraces that gapes for her.
Make the Earles bed readie, is the marriage done Sir?

Rut. Yes they are knit; but must this slubberdegullion Have her maiden-head now?

[*Char*.] There's no avoiding it.

Rut. And there's the scaffold where she must lose it.

[*Char*.] The bed Sir.

Rut. No way to wipe his mouldy chaps?

Char. That we know.

Rut. To any honest well-deserving fellow,
And 'twere but to a merry Cobbler, I could sit still now,
I love the game so well; but that this puckfist,
This universal rutter—fare ye well Sir;
And if you have any good prayers, put 'em forward,
There may be yet a remedie.

Char. I wish it, [*Exit* Rut. And all my best devotions offer to it.

Enter Clodio, *and* Guard.

Clod. Now is this tye dispatch'd?

Char. I think it be Sir.

Clod. And my bed ready?

Char. There you may quickly find Sir, Such a loath'd preparation.

Clod. Never grumble,
Nor fling a discontent upon my pleasure,
It must and shall be done: give me some wine,
And fill it till it leap upon my lips: [*wine*
Here's to the foolish maidenhead you wot of,
The toy I must take pains for.

Char. I beseech your Lordship Load not a Fathers love.

Clod. Pledge it *Charino*,
Or by my life I'le make thee pledge thy last,
And be sure she be a maid, a perfect Virgin,
(I will not have my expectation dull'd)
Or your old pate goes off. I am hot and fiery,
And my bloud beats alarms through my body,
And fancie high. You of my guard retire,
And let me hear no noise about the lodging
But musick and sweet ayres, now fetch your Daughter,
And bid the coy wench put on all her beauties,
All her enticements, out-blush damask Roses,
And dim the breaking East with her bright Crystals.
I am all on fire, away.

Char. And I am frozen. [*Exit*.

Enter Zenocia *with Bow and Quiver, an Arrow bent*, Arnoldo *and* Rutilio *after her, arm'd*.

Zen. Come fearless on.

Rut. Nay an I budge from thee Beat me with durty sticks.

Clod. What Masque is this?
What pretty fancy to provoke me high?
The beauteous Huntress, fairer far, and sweeter;
Diana shewes an Ethiop to this beauty
Protected by two Virgin Knights.

Rut. That's a lye, A loud one, if you knew as much as I do, The Guard's dispers'd.

Arn. Fortune I hope invites us.

Clod. I can no longer hold, she pulls my heart from me.

Zen. Stand, and stand fixt, move not a foot, nor speak not,
For if thou doest, upon this point thy death sits.
Thou miserable, base, and sordid lecher,
Thou scum of noble blood, repent and speedily,
Repent thy thousand thefts, from helpless Virgins,
Their innocence betrayed to thy embraces.

Arn. The base dishonour, that thou doest to strangers,
In glorying to abuse the Laws of Marriage,
Thy Infamy thou hast flung upon thy Country,
In nourishing this black and barbarous Custom.

Clod. My Guard.

Arn. One word more, and thou diest.

Rut. One syllable
That tends to any thing, but I beseech you,
And as y'are Gentlemen tender my case,
And I'le thrust my Javeling down thy throat.
Thou Dog-whelp, thou, pox upon thee, what
Should I call thee, Pompion,
Thou kiss my Lady? thou scour her Chamber-pot:
Thou have a Maiden-head? a mottly Coat,
You great blind fool, farewel and be hang'd to ye,
Lose no time Lady.

Arn. Pray take your pleasure Sir, And so we'l take our leaves.

Zen. We are determined, Dye, before yield.

Arn. Honour, and a fair grave.

Zen. Before a lustful Bed, so for our fortunes.

Rut. *Du cat awhee*, good Count, cry, prethee cry, O what a wench hast thou lost! cry you great booby. [*Exe*.

Enter Charino.

Clod. And is she gone then, am I dishonoured thus,
Cozened and baffl'd? my Guard there, no man answer?
My Guard I say, sirrah you knew of this plot;
Where are my Guard? I'le have your life you villain,
You politick old Thief.

Char. Heaven send her far enough,

Enter Guard.

And let me pay the ransom.

Guard. Did your honour call us?

Clod. Post every way, and presently recover The two strange Gentlemen, and the fair Lady.

Guard. This day was Married Sir?

Clod. The same.

Guard. We saw 'em. Making with all main speed to th' Port.

Clod. Away villains. [*Exit Guard*. Recover her, or I shall dye; deal truly, Didst not thou know?

Char. By all that's good I did not. If your honour mean their flight, to say I grieve for that, Will be to lye; you may handle me as you please.

Clod. Be sure, with all the cruelty, with all the rigor, For thou hast rob'd me villain of a treasure.

Enter Guard.

How now?

Guard. They're all aboard, a Bark rode ready for 'em, And now are under Sail, and past recovery.

Clod. Rig me a Ship with all the speed that may be,
I will not lose her: thou her most false Father,
Shalt go along; and if I miss her, hear me,
A whole day will I study to destroy thee.

Char. I shall be joyful of it; and so you'l find me.

[*Exeunt omnes.*

Actus Secundus. Scena Prima.

Enter Manuel du Sosa, *and* Guiomar.

Man. I Hear and see too much of him, and that
Compels me Madam, though unwillingly,
To wish I had no Uncles part in him,
And much I fear, the comfort of a Son
You will not long enjoy.

Gui. 'Tis not my fault,
And therefore from his guilt my innocence
Cannot be tainted, since his Fathers death,
(Peace to his soul) a Mothers prayers and care
Were never wanting, in his education.
His Child-hood I pass o're, as being brought up
Under my wing; and growing ripe for study,
I overcame the tenderness, and joy
I had to look upon him, and provided
The choicest Masters, and of greatest name
Of *Salamanca*, in all liberal Arts.

Man. To train his youth up. I must witness that.

Gui. How there he prospered to the admiration
Of all that knew him, for a general Scholar,
Being one of note, before he was a man,
Is still remembred in that *Academy*,
From thence I sent him to the Emperours Court,
Attended like his Fathers Son, and there
Maintain'd him, in such bravery and height,
As did become a Courtier.

Man. 'Twas that spoil'd him, my Nephew had been happy.
The Court's a School indeed, in which some few
Learn vertuous principles, but most forget
What ever they brought thither good and honest.
Trifling is there in practice, serious actions
Are obsolete and out of use, my Nephew
Had been a happy man, had he ne're known
What's there in grace and fashion.

Gui. I have heard yet,
That while he liv'd in Court, the Emperour
Took notice of his carriage and good parts,
The Grandees did not scorn his company,
And of the greatest Ladies he was held
A compleat Gentleman.

Man. He indeed Daunc'd well;
A turn o'th' Toe, with a lofty trick or two,
To argue nimbleness, and a strong back,
Will go far with a Madam: 'tis most true,
That he's an excellent Scholar, and he knows it;
An exact Courtier, and he knows that too;
He has fought thrice, and come off still with honour,
Which he forgets not.

Gui. Nor have I much reason, To grieve his fortune that way.

Man. You are mistaken,
Prosperity does search a Gentlemans temper,
More than his adverse fortune: I have known
Many, and of rare parts from their success
In private Duels, rais'd up to such a pride,
And so transform'd from what they were, that all
That lov'd them truly, wish'd they had fallen in them.
I need not write examples, in your Son
'Tis too apparent; for e're *Don Duarte*
Made tryal of his valour, he indeed was
Admired for civil courtesie, but now

He's swoln so high, out of his own assurance,
Of what he dares do, that he seeks occasions,
Unjust occasions, grounded on blind passion,
Ever to be in quarrels, and this makes him
Shunn'd of all fair Societies.

Gui. Would it were
In my weak power to help it: I will use
With my entreaties th' Authority of a Mother,
As you may of an Uncle, and enlarge it
With your command, as being a Governour
To the great King in _Lisbon.

Enter_ Duarte *and his Page*.

Man. Here he comes. We are unseen, observe him.

Dua. Boy.

Page. My Lord.

Dua. What saith the *Spanish* Captain that I struck, To my bold challenge?

Page. He refus'd to read it.

Dua. Why didst not leave it there?

Page. I did my Lord,
But to no purpose, for he seems more willing
To sit down with the wrongs, than to repair
His honour by the sword; he knows too well,
That from your Lordship nothing can be got
But more blows, and disgraces.

Dua. He's a wretch,
A miserable wretch, and all my fury
Is lost upon him; holds the Mask, appointed
I'th' honour of *Hippolyta*?

Page. 'Tis broke off.

Dua. The reason?

Page. This was one, they heard your Lordship
Was by the Ladies choice to lead the Dance,
And therefore they, too well assur'd how far
You would outshine 'em, gave it o're and said,
They would not serve for foiles to set you off.

Dua. They at their best are such, and ever shall be Where I appear.

Man. Do you note his modesty?

Dua. But was there nothing else pretended?

Page. Yes,
Young Don *Alonzo*, the great Captains Nephew,
Stood on comparisons.

Dua. With whom?

Page. With you,
And openly profess'd that all precedence,
His birth and state consider'd, was due to him,
Nor were your Lordship to contend with one
So far above you.

Dua. I look down upon him
With such contempt and scorn, as on my slave,
He's a name only, and all good in him
He must derive from his great grandsires Ashes,
For had not their victorious acts bequeath'd
His titles to him, and wrote on his forehead,
This is a Lord, he had liv'd unobserv'd
By any man of mark, and died as one
Amongst the common route. Compare with me?
'Tis Gyant-like ambition; I know him,
And know my self, that man is truly noble,
And he may justly call that worth his own,
Which his deserts have purchas'd, I could wish
My birth were more obscure, my friends and kinsmen

Of lesser power, or that my provident Father
Had been like to that riotous Emperour
That chose his belly for his only heir;
For being of no family then, and poor
My vertues wheresoe'r I liv'd, should make
That kingdom my inheritance.

Gui. Strange self Love!

Dua. For if I studied the Countries Laws,
I should so easily sound all their depth,
And rise up such a wonder, that the pleaders,
That now are in most practice and esteem,
Should starve for want of Clients: if I travell'd,
Like wise *Ulysses* to see men and manners,
I would return in act, more knowing, than
Homer could fancy him; if a Physician,
So oft I would restore death-wounded men,
That where I liv'd, *Galen* should not be nam'd,
And he that joyn'd again the scatter'd limbs
Of torn *Hippolytus* should be forgotten.
I could teach *Ovid* courtship, how to win
A *Julia*, and enjoy her, though her Dower
Were all the Sun gives light to: and for arms
Were the *Persian* host that drank up Rivers, added
To the *Turks* present powers, I could direct,
Command, and Marshal them.

Man. And yet you know not To rule your self, you would not to a boy else Like *Plautus* Braggart boast thus.

Dua. All I speak, In act I can make good.

Gui. Why then being Master
Of such and so good parts do you destroy them,
With self opinion, or like a rich miser,
Hoard up the treasures you possess, imparting
Nor to your self nor others, the use of them?
They are to you but like inchanted viands,

On which you seem to feed, yet pine with hunger;
And those so rare perfections in my Son
Which would make others happy, render me
A wretched Mother.

Man. You are too insolent.
And those too many excellencies, that feed
Your pride, turn to a Pleurisie, and kill
That which should nourish vertue; dare you think
All blessings are confer'd on you alone?
Y'are grosly cousen'd; there's no good in you,
Which others have not: are you a Scholar? so
Are many, and as knowing: are you valiant?
Waste not that courage then in braules, but spend it
In the Wars, in service of your King and Country.

Dua. Yes, so I might be General, no man lives That's worthy to command me.

Man. Sir, in *Lisbon*
I am: and you shall know it; every hour
I am troubled with complaints of your behaviour
From men of all conditions, and all sexes.
And my authority, which you presume
Will bear you out, in that you are my Nephew,
No longer shall protect you, for I vow
Though all that's past I pardon, I will punish
The next fault with as much severity
As if you were a stranger, rest assur'd on't.

Gui. And by that love you should bear, or that duty
You owe a Mother, once more I command you
To cast this haughtiness off; which if you do,
All that is mine, is yours, if not, expect
My prayers, and vows, for your conversion only,
But never means nor favour. [*Ex*. Manuel *and* Guiomar.

Dua. I am Tutor'd
As if I were a child still, the base Peasants
That fear, and envy my great worth, have done this;
But I will find them out, I will o'boord
Get my disguise; I have too long been idle,
Nor will I curb my spirit, I was born free,
And will pursue the course best liketh me. [*Exeunt.*

Enter Leopold, Sailers, *and* Zenocia.

Leop. Divide the spoil amongst you, this fair Captive I only challenge for my self.

Sail. You have won her
And well deserve her: twenty years I have liv'd
A Burgess of the Sea, and have been present
At many a desperate fight, but never saw
So small a Bark with such incredible valour
So long defended, and against such odds,
And by two men scarce arm'd too.

Leop. 'Twas a wonder.
And yet the courage they exprest being taken,
And their contempt of death wan more upon me
Than all they did, when they were free: me thinks
I see them yet when they were brought aboard us,
Disarm'd and ready to be put in fetters
How on the suddain, as if they had sworn
Never to taste the bread of servitude,
Both snatching up their swords, and from this Virgin,
Taking a farewel only with their eyes,
They leapt into the Sea.

Sail. Indeed 'twas rare.

Leop. It wrought so much on me, that but I fear'd
The great ship that pursued us, our own safety
Hindring my charitable purpose to 'em,
I would have took 'em up, and with their lives

They should have had their liberties.

Zen. O too late, For they are lost, for ever lost.

Leop. Take comfort
'Tis not impossible, but that they live yet,
For when they left the ships, they were within
A League o'th' shore, and with such strength and cunning
They swimming, did delude the rising Billows,
With one hand making way, and with the other,
Their bloudy swords advanced, threatning the Sea-gods
With war, unless they brought them safely off,
That I am almost confident they live,
And you again may see them.

Zen. In that hope
I brook a wretched being, till I am
Made certain of their fortunes; but they dead,
Death hath so many doors to let out life,
I will not long survive them.

Leop. Hope the best,
And let the courteous usage you have found,
Not usual in men of War perswade you
To tell me your condition.

Zen. You know it,
A Captive, my fate and your power have made me,
Such I am now, but what I was it skills not:
For they being dead, in whom I only live,
I dare not challenge Family, or Country,
And therefore Sir enquire not, let it suffice,
I am your servant, and a thankful servant
(If you will call that so, which is but duty)
I ever will be, and my honour safe,
Which nobly hitherto ye have preserv'd,
No slavery can appear in such a form,

Which with a masculine constancy I will not
Boldly look on and suffer.

Leop. You mistake me:
That you are made my prisoner, may prove
The birth of your good fortune. I do find
A winning language in your tongue and looks;
Nor can a suit by you mov'd be deni'd,
And therefore of a prisoner you must be
The Victors advocate.

Zen. To whom?

Leap. A Lady:
In whom all graces that can perfect beauty
Are friendly met. I grant that you are fair:
And had I not seen her before, perhaps
I might have sought to you.

Zen. This I hear gladly.

Leap. To this incomparable Lady I will give you,
(Yet being mine, you are already hers)
And to serve her is more than to be free,
At least I think so; and when you live with her,
If you will please to think on him that brought you
To such a happiness, for so her bounty
Will make you think her service, you shall ever
Make me at your devotion.

Zen. All I can do, Rest you assur'd of.

Leap. At night I'le present you, Till when I am your Guard.

Zen. Ever your servant. [*Exeunt.*

Enter Arnoldo *and* Rutilio.

Arn. To what are we reserv'd?

Rut. Troth 'tis uncertain,
Drowning we have scap'd miraculously, and
Stand fair for ought I know for hanging; mony
We have none, nor e're are like to have,
'Tis to be doubted: besides we are strangers,
Wondrous hungry strangers; and charity
Growing cold, and miracles ceasing,
Without a Conjurers help, cannot find
When we shall eat again.

Arn. These are no wants
If put in ballance with *Zenocias* loss;
In that alone all miseries are spoken:
O my *Rutilio,* when I think on her,
And that which she may suffer, being a Captive,
Then I could curse my self, almost those powers
That send me from the fury of the Ocean.

Rut. You have lost a wife indeed, a fair and chast one,
Two blessings, not found often in one woman;
But she may be recovered, questionless
The ship that took us was of *Portugal,*
And here in *Lisbon,* by some means or other
We may hear of her.

Arn. In that hope I live.

Rut. And so do I, but hope is a poor Sallad To dine and sup with, after a two dayes fast too, Have you no mony left?

Arn. Not a Denier.

Rut. Nor any thing to pawn? 'tis now in fashion, Having a Mistress, sure you should not be Without a neat Historical shirt.

Arn. For shame Talk not so poorly.

Rut. I must talk of that
Necessity prompts us to, for beg I cannot,
Nor am I made to creep in at a window,

To filch to feed me, something must be done,
And suddenly resolve on't.

Enter Zabulon *and a Servant.*

Arn. What are these?

Rut. One by his habit is a *Jew.*

Zab. No more: Thou art sure that's he.

Ser. Most certain.

Zab. How long is it Since first she saw him?

Ser. Some two hours.

Zab. Be gone—let me alone to work him. [*Exit* Ser.

Rut. How he eyes you! Now he moves towards us, in the Devils name What would he with us?

Arn. Innocence is bold: Nor can I fear.

Zab. That you are poor and strangers, I easily perceive.

Rut. But that you'l help us, Or any of your tribe, we dare not hope Sir.

Zab. Why think you so?

Rut. Because you are a *Jew* Sir, And courtesies come sooner from the Devil Than any of your Nation.

Zab. We are men,
And have like you, compassion when we find
Fit subjects for our bounty, and for proof
That we dare give, and freely, not to you Sir,
Pray spare your pains, there's gold, stand not amaz'd,
'Tis current I assure you.

Rut. Take it man,
Sure thy good Angel is a *Jew*, and comes
In his own shape to help thee: I could wish now
Mine would appear too like a *Turk.*

Arn. I thank you,
But yet must tell you, if this be the Prologue
To any bad act, you would have me practise,
I must not take it.

Zab. This is but the earnest
Of [t]hat which is to follow, and the bond
Which you must seal to for't, is your advancement,
Fortune with all that's in her power to give,
Offers her self up to you: entertain her,
And that which Princes have kneel'd for in vain
Presents it self to you.

Arn. 'Tis above wonder.

Zab. But far beneath the truth, in my relation
Of what you shall possess, if you emb[r]ace it.
There is an hour in each mans life appointed
To make his happiness if then he seize it,
And this, (in which, beyond all expectation,
You are invited to your good) is yours,
If you dare follow me, so, if not, hereafter
Expect not the like offer. [*Exit*.

Arn. 'Tis no vision.

Rut. 'Tis gold I'm sure.

Arn. We must like brothers share; There's for you.

Rut. By this light I'm glad I have it:
There are few Gallants, (for men may be such
And yet want gold, yea and sometimes silver)
But would receive such favours from the Devil,
Though he appear'd like a Broker, and demanded
Sixty i'th' hundred.

Arn. Wherefore should I fear
Some plot upon my life? 'tis now to me

Not worth the keeping. I will follow him,
Farewel, wish me good fortune, we shall meet
Again I doubt not.

Rut. Or I'le ne're trust *Jew* more, [*Exit* Arnoldo. Nor Christian for his sake—plague o' my stars, How long might I have walkt without a Cloak, Before I should have met with such a fortune? We elder Brothers, though we are proper men, *Ha' not the luck*, ha' too much beard, that spoils us; The smooth Chin carries all: what's here to do now? [*Manet* Rutilio.

Enter Duarte, Alonzo, *and a* Page.

Dua. I'le take you as I find you.

Alon. That were base—you see I am unarm'd.

Dua. Out with your Bodkin
Your Pocket-dagger, your Steletto, out with it,
Or by this hand I'le kill you: such as you are
Have studied the undoing of poor Cutlers,
And made all manly weapons out of fashion:
You carry Poniards to murder men,
Yet dare not wear a sword to guard your Honour.

Rut. That's true indeed: upon my life this gallant Is brib'd to repeal banisht swords.

Dua. I'le shew you The difference now between a *Spanish* Rapier And your pure Pisa.

Alon. Let me fetch a sword, Upon mine honour I'le return.

Dua. Not so Sir.

Alon. Or lend me yours I pray you, and take this.

Rut. To be disgrac'd as you are, no I thank you
Spight of the fashion, while I live, I am
Instructed to go arm'd: what folly 'tis
For you that are a man, to put your self
Into your enemies mercy.

Dua. Yield it quickly
Or I'le cut off your hand, and now disgrace you,
Thus kick and baffle you: as you like this,
You may again prefer complaints against me
To my Uncle and my Mother, and then think
To make it good with a Poniard.

Alon. I am paid For being of the fashion.

Dua. Get a sword,
Then if you dare redeem your reputation:
You know I am easily found: I'le add this to it
To put you in mind.

Rut. You are too insolent,
And do insult too much on the advantage
Of that which your unequal weapon gave you,
More than your valour.

Dua. This to me, you Peasant?
Thou art not worthy of my foot poor fellow,
'Tis scorn, not pity, makes me give thee life:
Kneel down and thank me for't: how, do you stare?

Rut. I have a sword Sir, you shall find, a good one; This is no stabbing guard.

Dua. Wert thou thrice arm'd, Thus yet I durst attempt thee.

Rut. Then have at you, [*Fight.* I scorn to take blows.

Dua. O I am slain. [*Falls.*

Page. Help! murther, murther!

Alon. Shift for your self you are dead else, You have kill'd the Governou[r]s Nephew.

Page. Raise the streets there.

Alon. If once you are beset you cannot scape, Will you betray your self?

Rut. Undone for ever. [*Exit* Rut. *and* Alonzo.

Enter Officers.

1 Off. Who makes this out-cry?

Page. O my Lord is murdered; This way he took, make after him, Help help there. [*Exit* Page.

2 Offi. 'Tis *Don Duarte*.

1 Offi. Pride has got a fall,
He was still in quarrels, scorn'd us Peace-makers,
And all our Bill-authority, now h'as paid for't.
You ha' met with your match Sir now, bring off his body
And bear it to the Governour. Some pursue
The murderer; yet if he scape, it skills not;
Were I a Prince, I would reward him for't,
He has rid the City of a turbulent beast,
There's few will pity him: but for his Mother
I truly grieve indeed, she's a good Lady. [*Exeunt*.

Enter Guiomar *and* Servants.

Gui. He's not i'th' house?

_Ser. No Madam.

Gui. Haste and seek him,
Go all and every where, Pie not to bed
Till you return him, take away the lights too,
The Moon lends me too much, to find my fears
And those devotions I am to pay
Are written in my heart, not in this book, [*Kneel*.
And I shall read them there without a Taper. [*Ex*. Ser.

Enter Rutilio.

Rut. I am pursued; all the Ports are stopt too;
Not any hope to escape, behind, before me,
On either side I am beset, cursed fortune
My enemie on the Sea, and on the Land too,
Redeem'd from one affliction to another:

Would I had made the greedy waves my tomb
And dyed obscure, and innocent, not as Nero
Smear'd o're with blood. Whither have my fears brought me?
I am got into a house, the doors all open,
This, by the largeness of the room, the hangings,
And other rich adornments, glistring through
The sable masque of night, sayes it belongs
To one of means and rank: no servant stirring?
Murmur nor whisper?

Guio. Who's that?

Rut. By the voice, This is a woman.

Guio. Stephana, Jaspe, Julia, Who waits there?

Rut. 'Tis the Lady of the house, I'le flie to her protection.

Guio. Speak, what are you?

Rut. Of all that ever breath'd, a man most wretched.

Guio. I am sure you are a man of most ill manners,
You could not with so little reverence else
Press to my private chamber. Whither would you,
Or what do you seek for?

Rut. Gracious woman hear me;
I am a stranger, and in that I answer
All your demands, a most unfortunate stranger,
That call'd unto it by my enemies pride,
Have left him dead i'th' streets, Justice pursues me,
And for that life I took unwillingly,
And in a fair defence, I must lose mine,
Unless you in your charity protect me.
Your house is now my sanctuary, and the Altar,
I gladly would take hold of your sweet mercy.
By all that's dear unto you, by your vertues,
And by your innocence, that needs no forgiveness,
Take pity on me.

Guio. Are you a *Castillian*?

Rut. No Madam, *Italy* claims my birth.

Guio. I ask not
With purpose to betray you, if you were
Ten thousand times a Spaniard, the nation
We Portugals most hate, I yet would save you
If it lay in my power: lift up these hangings;
Behind my Beds head there's a hollow place,
Into which enter; so, but from this stir not
If the Officers come, as you expect they will doe,
I know they owe such reverence to my lodgings,
That they will easily give credit to me
And search no further.

Rut. The blest Saints pay for me The infinite debt I owe you.

Guio. How he quakes!
Thus far I feel his heart beat, be of comfort,
Once more I give my promise for your safety,
All men are subject to such accidents,
Especially the valiant; and who knows not,
But that the charity I afford this stranger
My only Son else where may stand in need of?

Enter Officers, and Servants, with the body of Duarte – Page.

1 Ser. Now Madam, if your wisedom ever could
Raise up defences against floods of sorrow
That haste to overwhelm you, make true use of
Your great discretion.

2 Ser. Your only son My Lord *Duart's* slain.

1 Off. His murtherer, pursued by us
Was by a boy discovered
Entring your house, and that induced us
To press into it for his apprehension.

Guio. Oh!

1 Ser. Sure her heart is broke.

Off. Madam.

Guio. Stand off.
My sorrow is so dear and pretious to me,
That you must not partake it, suffer it
Like wounds that do breed inward to dispatch me.
O my *Duart*, such an end as this
Thy pride long since did prophesie; thou art dead,
And to encrease my misery, thy sad Mother
Must make a wilfull shipwrack of her vow
Or thou fall unreveng'd. My Soul's divided,
And piety to a son, and true performance
Of hospitable duties to my guest,
That are to others Angels, are my furies.
Vengeance knocks at my heart, but my word given
Denies the entrance, is no *Medium* left,
But that I must protect the murderer,
Or suffer in that faith he made his altar?
Motherly love give place, the fault made this way,
To keep a vow, to which high Heaven is witness,
Heaven may be pleas'd to pardon.

Enter Manuel, Doctors, Surgeons.

Man. 'Tis too late,
Hee's gone, past all recovery: now reproof
Were but unseasonable when I should give comfort,
And yet remember Sister.

Guio. O forbear,
Search for the murtherer, and remove the body,
And as you think fit, give it burial.
Wretch that I am, uncapable of all comfort,
And therefore I intreat my friends and kinsfolk,
And you my Lord, for some space to forbear

Your courteous visitations.

Man. We obey you. [*Exeunt omnes with the body.* Manet Guiomar.

Rut. My Spirits come back, and now despair resigns Her place again to hope.

Guio. What ere thou art
To whom I have given means of life, to witness
With what Religion I have kept my promise,
Come fearless forth, but let thy face be cover'd,
That I hereafter be not forc't to know thee,
For motherly affection may return
My vow once paid to heaven. Thou hast taken from me
The respiration of my heart, the light
Of my swoln eyes, in his life that sustain'd me:
Yet my word given to save you, I make good,
Because what you did, was not done with malice,
You are not known, there is no mark about you
That can discover you; let not fear betray you.
With all convenient speed you can, flie from me
That I may never see you; and that want
Of means may be no let unto your journie,
There are a hundred Crownes: you are at the door now,
And so Farewell for ever.

Rut. Let me first fall
Before your feet, and on them pay the duty
I owe your goodness; next all blessings to you,
And Heaven restore the joyes I have bereft you,
With full increase hereafter, living be
The Goddess stil'd of Hospitalitie.

Actus Tertius. Scena Prima.

Enter Leopold, and Zenocia.

Leo. Fling off these sullen clouds, you are enter'd now Into a house of joy and happiness, I have prepar'd a blessing for ye.

Zen. Thank ye, my state would rather ask a curse.

Leo. You are peevish
And know not when ye are friended, I have us'd those means,
The Lady of this house, the noble Lady,
Will take ye as her own, and use ye graciously:
Make much of what you are, Mistris of that beautie,
And expose it not to such betraying sorrows,
When ye are old, and all those sweets hang wither'd,

Enter Servant.

Then sit and sigh.

Zen. My *Autumn* is not far off.

Leo. Have you told your Lady?

Ser. Yes Sir, I have told her Both of your noble service, and your present, Which she accepts.

Leo. I should be blest to see her.

Ser. That now you cannot doe: she keeps the Chamber
Not well dispos'd; and has denied all visits,
The maid I have in charge to receive from ye,
So please you render her.

Leo. With all my service, But fain I would have seen.

Ser. 'Tis but your patience; No doubt she cannot but remember nobly.

Leo. These three years I have lov'd this scornfull Lady,
And follow'd her with all the truth of service,
In all which time, but twice she has honour'd me
With sight of her blest beauty: when you please Sir,
You may receive your charge, and tell your Lady;
A Gentleman whose life is only dedicated

To her commands, kisses her beauteous hands;
And Faire-one, now your help, you may remember
The honest courtesies, since you are mine,
I ever did your modestie: you shall be near her,
And if sometimes you name my service to her,
And tell her with what nobleness I love her,
'Twill be a gratitude I shall remember.

Zen. What in my poor power lyes, so it be honest.

Leo. I ask no more.

Ser. You must along with me (Fair.)

Leo. And so I leave you two: but a fortune Too happy for my fate: you shall enjoy her.

Scena Secunda.

Enter Zabulon and Servants.

Zab. Be quick, be quick, out with the banquet there, These scents are dull; cast richer on, and fuller; Scent every place, where have you plac'd the musick?

Ser. Here they stand ready Sir.

Zab. 'Tis well, be sure The wines be lusty, high, and full of Spirit, And Amber'd all.

Ser. They are.

Zab. Give fair attendance. In the best trim, and state, make ready all. I shall come presently again. [*Banquet set forth. Exit.*

2 Ser. We shall Sir,
What preparation's this?
Some new device

My Lady has in hand.

1 Ser. O, prosper it As long as it carries good wine in the mouth, And good meat with it, where are all the rest?

2 Ser. They are ready to attend. [*Musick.*

1 Ser. Sure some great person, They would not make this hurry else.

2 Ser. Hark the Musick.

Enter Zabulon, *and* Arnoldo.

It will appear now certain, here it comes.
Now to our places.

Arn. Whither will he lead me?
What invitation's this? to what new end
Are these fair preparations? a rich Banquet,
Musick, and every place stuck with adornment,
Fit for a Princes welcome; what new game
Has Fortune now prepar'd to shew me happy?
And then again to sink me? 'tis no illusion,
Mine eyes are not deceiv'd, all these are reall;
What wealth and state!

Zab. Will you sit down and eat Sir?
These carry little wonder, they are usual;
But you shall see, if you be wise to observe it,
That that will strike dead, strike with amazement,
Then if you be a man: this fair health to you.

Ar. What shall I see? I pledge ye Sir, I was never So buried in amazement—

Zab. You are so still: Drink freely.

Ar. The very wines are admirable:
Good Sir, give me leave to ask this question,
For what great worthy man are these prepar'd?

And why do you bring me hither?

Zab. They are for you, Sir;
And under-value not the worth you carry,
You are that worthy man: think well of these,
They shall be more, and greater.

Ar. Well, blind fortune Thou hast the prettiest changes when thou art pleas'd, To play thy game out wantonly—

Zab. Come be lusty, And awake your Spirits. [*Cease Musick.*

Ar. Good Sir, do not wake me. For willingly I would dye in this dream, pray whose Servants Are all these that attend here?

Zab. They are yours; They wait on you.

Ar. I never yet remember I kept such faces, nor that I was ever able To maintain so many.

Zab. Now you are, and shall be.

Ar. You'l say this house is mine too?

Zab. Say it? swear it.

Ar. And all this wealth?

Zab. This is the least you see Sir.

Ar. Why, where has this been hid these thirtie years?
For certainly I never found I was wealthie
Till this hour, never dream'd of house, and Servants.
I had thought I had been a younger Brother, a poor Gent.
I may eat boldly then.

Zab. 'Tis prepar'd for ye.

Ar. The taste is perfect, and most delicate:
But why for me? give me some wine, I do drink;
I feel it sensibly, and I am here,
Here in this glorious place: I am bravely us'd too,
Good Gentle Sir, give me leave to think a little,

For either I am much abus'd—

Zab. Strike Musick And sing that lusty Song. [*Musick. Song.*

Ar. Bewitching harmony! Sure I am turn'd into another Creature.

Enter Hippolyta.

Happy and blest, *Arnoldo* was unfortunate;
Ha! bless mine eyes; what pretious piece of nature
To pose the world?

Zab. I told you, you would see that Would darken these poor preparations; What think ye now? nay rise not, 'tis no vision.

Ar. 'Tis more: 'tis miracle.

Hip. You are welcom Sir.

Ar. It speaks, and entertains me still more glorious; She is warm, and this is flesh here: how she stirs me! Bless me what stars are there?

Hip. May I sit near ye?

Ar. No, you are too pure an object to behold, Too excellent to look upon, and live; I must remove.

Zab. She is a woman Sir, Fy, what faint heart is this?

Arn. The house of wonder.

Zab. Do not you think your self now truly happy?
You have the abstract of all sweetness by ye,
The precious wealth youth labours to arrive at;
Nor is she less in honour, than in beauty,
Ferrara's Royal Duke is proud to call her
His best, his Noblest, and most happy Sister,
Fortune has made her Mistress of herself,
Wealthy, and wise, without a power to sway her,
Wonder of *Italy*, of all hearts Mistress.

Arn. And all this is—

Zab. Hippolyta the beauteous.

Hip. You are a poor relator of my fortunes,
Too weak a Chronicle to speak my blessings,
And leave out that essential part of story
I am most high and happy in, most fortunate,
The acquaintance, and the noble fellowship
Of this fair Gentleman: pray ye do not wonder,
Nor hold it strange to hear a handsome Lady
Speak freely to ye: with your fair leave and courtesie
I will sit by ye.

Arn. I know not what to answer, Nor where I am, nor to what end consider; Why do you use me thus?

Hip. Are ye angry Sir, Because ye are entertain'd with all humanity? Freely and nobly us'd?

Arn. No gentle Lady,
That were uncivil, but it much amazes me
A stranger, and a man of no desert
Should find such floods of courtesie.

Hip. I love ye,
I honour ye, the first and best of all men,
And where that fair opinion leads, 'tis usual
These trifles that but serve to set off, follow.
I would not have you proud now, nor disdainful
Because I say I love ye, though I swear it,
Nor think it a stale favour I fling on ye,
Though ye be handsome, and the only man
I must confess I ever fixt mine eye on,
And bring along all promises that please us,
Yet I should hate ye then, despise ye, scorn ye,
And with as much contempt pursue your person,
As now I do with love. But you are wiser,
At least I think, more master of your fortune,
And so I drink your health.

Arn. Hold fast good honesty, I am a lost man else.

Hip. Now you may kiss me, 'Tis the first kiss, I ever askt, I swear to ye.

Arn. That I dare do sweet Lady.

Hip. You do it well too; You are a Master Sir, that makes you coy.

Arn. Would you would send your people off.

Hip. Well thought on. Wait all without. [*Exit* Zab. *and Servants.*

Zab. I hope she is pleas'd throughly.

Hip. Why stand ye still? here's no man to detect ye,
My people are gone off: come, come, leave conjuring,
The Spirit you would raise, is here already,
Look boldly on me.

Arn. What would you have me do?

Hip. O most unmanly question! have you do? Is't possible your years should want a Tutor? I'le teach ye: come, embrace me.

Arn. Fye stand off;
And give me leave, more now than e're, to wonder,
A building of so goodly a proportion,
Outwardly all exact, the frame of Heaven,
Should hide within so base inhabitants?
You are as fair, as if the morning bare ye,
Imagination never made a sweeter;
Can it be possible this frame should suffer,
And built on slight affections, fright the viewer?
Be excellent in all, as you are outward,
The worthy Mistress of those many blessings
Heaven has bestowed, make 'em appear still nobler,
Because they are trusted to a weaker keeper.
Would ye have me love ye?

Hip. Yes.

Arn. Not for your beauty;
Though I confess, it blowes the first fire in us,

Time as he passes by, puts out that sparkle;
Nor for your wealth, although the world kneel to it,
And make it all addition to a woman,
Fortune that ruines all, makes that his conquest;
Be honest, and be vertuous, I'le admire ye,
At least be wise, and where ye lay these nets,
Strow over 'em a little modesty,
'Twill well become your cause, and catch more Fools.

Hip. Could any one that lov'd this wholesome counsel
But love the giver more? you make me fonder:
You have a vertuous mind, I want that ornament;
Is it a sin I covet to enjoy ye?
If ye imagine I am too free a Lover,
And act that part belongs to you, I am silent:
Mine eyes shall speak my blushes, parly with ye;
I will not touch your hand, but with a tremble
Fitting a Vestal Nun; not long to kiss ye,
But gently as the Air, and undiscern'd too,
I'le steal it thus: I'le walk your shadow by ye,
So still and silent that it shall be equal,
To put me off, as that, and when I covet,
To give such toyes as these—

Arn. A new temptation—

Hip. Thus like the lazie minutes will I drop 'em, Which past once are forgotten.

Arn. Excellent vice!

Hip. Will ye be won? look stedfastly upon me,
Look manly, take a mans affections to you;
Young women, in the old world were not wont, Sir,
To hang out gaudy bushes for their beauties,
To talk themselves into young mens affections;
How cold and dull you are!

Arn. How I stagger! She is wise, as fair; but 'tis a wicked wisdom; I'le choak before I yield.

Hip. Who waits within there? [Zabulon *within.* Make ready the green Chamber.

Zab. It shall be Madam.

Arn. I am afraid she will injoy me indeed.

Hip. What Musick do ye love?

Arn. A modest tongue.

Hip. We'l have enough of that: fye, fye, how lumpish! In a young Ladyes arms thus dull?

Arn. For Heaven sake Profess a little goodness.

Hip. Of what Country?

Arn. I am of *Rome.*

Hip. Nay then I know you mock me, The *Italians* are not frighted with such bug-bears, Prethee go in.

Arn. I am not well.

Hip. I'le make thee, I'le kiss thee well.

Arn. I am not sick of that sore.

Hip. Upon my Conscience, I must ravish thee, I shall be famous for the first example: With this I'le tye ye first, then try your strength Sir.

Arn. My strength? away base woman, I abhor thee. I am not caught with stales, disease dwell with thee. [*Exit.*

Hip. Are ye so quick? and have I lost my wishes? Hoe, *Zabulon*; my servants.

Enter Zabulon *and* Servants.

Zab. Call'd ye Madam?

Hip. Is all that beauty scorned, so many su'd for; So many Princes? by a stranger too? Must I endure this?

Zab. Where's the Gentleman?

Hip. Go presently, pursue the stranger, *Zabulon*.
He has broke from me, Jewels I have given him:
Charge him with theft: he has stoln my love, my freedome,
Draw him before the Governour, imprison him,
Why dost thou stay?

Zab. I'le teach him a new dance,
For playing fast and loose with such a Lady.
Come fellows, come: I'le execute your anger,
And to the full.

Hip. His scorn shall feel my vengeance. – [*Exeunt*.

Scena Tertia.

Enter Sulpicia *and* Jaques.

Sul. Shall I never see a lusty man again?

Ja. Faith Mistress You do so over-labour 'em when you have 'em, And so dry-founder 'em, they cannot last.

Sul. Where's the *French*-man?

Ja. Alas, he's all to fitters, and lyes, taking the height of his fortune with a Syringe. He's chin'd, he's chin'd good man, he is a mourner.

Sul. What's become of the *Dane*?

Ja. Who? goldy-locks?
He's foul i'th' touch-hole; and recoils again,
The main Spring's weaken'd that holds up his cock,
He lies at the sign of the *Sun*, to be new breech'd.

Sul. The Rutter too, is gone.

Ja. O that was a brave Rascal,
He would labour like a Thrasher: but alas
What thing can ever last? he has been ill mew'd,
And drawn too soon; I have seen him in the Hospital.

Sul. There was an *English*-man.

Ja. I there was an *English*-man;
You'l scant find any now, to make that name good:
There were those *English* that were men indeed,
And would perform like men, but now they are vanisht:
They are so taken up in their own Country,
And so beaten of their speed by their own women,
When they come here, they draw their legs like Hackneys:
Drink, and their own devices have undone 'em.

Sul. I must have one that's strong, no life in *Lisbon* else,
Perfect and young: my Custom with young Ladies,
And high fed City dames, will fall, and break else.
I want my self too, in mine age to nourish me:
They are all sunk I mantain'd: now what's this business,
What goodly fellow's that?

Enter Rutilio *and* Officers.

Rut. Why do you drag me? Pox o' your justice; let me loose.

1 Offi. Not so Sir.

Rut. Cannot a man fall into one of your drunken Cellars, And venture the breaking on's neck, your trap-doors open, But he must be us'd thus rascally?

1 Offi. What made you wandring So late i'th' night? you know that is imprisonment.

Rut. May be I walk in my sleep.

2 Offi. May be we'l walk ye. What made you wandring Sir, into that vault Where all the City store, and the Munition lay?

Rut. I fell into it by chance, I broke my shins for't:
Your worships feel not that: I knockt my head
Against a hundred posts, would you had had it.
Cannot I break my neck in my own defence?

2 Offi. This will not serve: you cannot put it off so, Your coming thither was to play the villain, To fire the Powder, to blow up that part o'th' City.

Rut. Yes, with my nose: why were the trap-doors open? Might not you fall, or you, had you gone that way? I thought your City had sunk.

1 Offi. You did your best Sir,
We must presume, to help it into th' Air,
If you call that sinking: we have told you what's the law,
He that is taken there, unless a Magistrate,
And have command in that place, presently
If there be nothing found apparent near him
Worthy his torture, or his present death,
Must either pay his fine for his presumption,
(Which is six hundred Duckets) or for six years
Tug at an Oar i'th' Gallies: will ye walk Sir,
For we presume you cannot pay the penalty.

Rut. Row in the Gallies, after all this mischief?

2 Offi. May be you were drunk, they'l keep you sober there.

Rut. Tug at an Oar? you are not arrant rascals, To catch me in a pit-fall, and betray me?

Sul. A lusty minded man.

Ja. A wondrous able.

Sul. Pray Gentlemen, allow me but that liberty To speak a few words with your prisoner, And I shall thank you.

1 Offi. Take your pleasure Lady.

Sul. What would you give that woman should redeem ye, Redeem ye from this slavery?

Rut. Besides my service I would give her my whole self, I would be her vassal.

Sul. She has reason to expect as much, considering
The great sum she pays for't, yet take comfort,
What ye shall do to merit this, is easie,
And I will be the woman shall befriend ye,
'Tis but to entertain some handsome Ladies,
And young fair Gentlewomen: you guess the way:
But giving of your mind—

Rut. I am excellent at it: You cannot pick out such another living. I understand ye: is't not thus?

Sul. Ye have it.

Rut. Bring me a hundred of 'em: I'le dispatch 'em.
I will be none but yours: should another offer
Another way to redeem me, I should scorn it.
What women you shall please: I am monstrous lusty:
Not to be taken down: would you have Children?
I'le get you those as fast, and thick as flie-blows.

Sul. I admire him: wonder at him!

Rut. Hark ye Lady, You may require sometimes—

Sul. I by my faith.

Rut. And you shall have it by my faith, and handsomly:
This old Cat will suck shrewdly: you have no Daughters?
I flye at all: now am I in my Kingdom.
Tug at an Oar? no, tug in a Feather-bed,
With good warm Caudles; hang your bread and water,
I'le make you young again, believe that Lady.
I will so frubbish you.

Sul. Come, follow Officers, This Gentleman is free: I'le pay the Duckets.

Rut. And when you catch me in your City-powdring-tub Again, boil me with Cabbidge.

1 Offi. You are both warn'd and arm'd Sir. [*Exeunt.*

Scena Quarta.

Enter Leopold, Hippolyta, Zenocia.

Zen. Will your Ladyship wear this Dressing?

Hip. Leave thy prating: I care not what I wear.

Zen. Yet 'tis my duty To know your pleasure, and my worst affliction To see you discontented.

Hip. Weeping too?
Prethee forgive me: I am much distemper'd,
And speak I know not what: to make thee amends
The Gown that I wore yesterday, is thine;
Let it alone awhile.

Leo. Now you perceive, And taste her bounty.

Zen. Much above my merit.

Leo. But have you not yet found a happy time To move for me.

Zen. I have watched all occasions, But hitherto, without success: yet doubt not But I'le embrace the first means.

Leo. Do, and prosper:
Excellent creature, whose perfections make
Even sorrow lovely, if your frowns thus take me,
What would your smiles doe?

Hip. Pox o' this stale Courtship: If I have any power.

Leo. I am commanded, Obedience is the Lovers sacrifice Which I pay gladly.

Hip. To be forc'd to wooe,
Being a woman, could not but torment me,
But bringing for my advocates, youth and beauty,
Set off with wealth, and then to be deni'd too
Do's comprehend all tortures. They flatter'd me,
That said my looks were charms, my touches fetters,
My locks soft chains, to bind the arms of Princes,
And make them in that wish'd for bondage, happy.
I am like others of a coarser feature,
As weak to allure, but in my dotage, stronger:
I am no *Circe*; he, more than *Ulysses*,
Scorns all my offer'd bounties, slights my favours,
And, as I were some new Egyptian, flyes me,
Leaving no pawn, but my own shame behind him.
But he shall finde, that in my fell revenge,
I am a woman: one that never pardons
The rude contemner of her proffered sweetness.

Enter Zabulon.

Zab. Madam, 'tis done.

Hip. What's done?

Zab. The uncivill stranger Is at your suite arrested.

Hip. 'Tis well handled.

Zab. And under guard sent to the Governour,
With whom my testimony, and the favour
He bears your Ladiship, have so prevail'd
That he is sentenc'd.

Hip. How?

Zab. To lose his head.

Hip. Is that the means to quench the scorching heat
Of my inrag'd desires? must innocence suffer,
'Cause I am faulty? or is my Love so fatall
That of necessity it must destroy
The object it most longs for? dull *Hippolyta*,

To think that injuries could make way for love,
When courtesies were despis'd: that by his death
Thou shouldst gain that, which only thou canst hope for
While he is living: My honour's at the stake now,
And cannot be preserv'd, unless he perish,
The enjoying of the thing I love, I ever
Have priz'd above my fame: why doubt I now then?
One only way is left me, to redeem all:
Make ready my Caroch.

Leo. What will you Madam?

Hip. And yet I am impatient of such stay:
Bind up my hair: fye, fye, while that is doing
The Law may seise his life: thus as I am then,
Not like *Hippolyta,* but a *Bacchanal*
My frantique Love transports me. [*Exit.*

Leo. Sure she's distracted.

Zab. Pray you follow her: I will along with you:
I more than ghess the cause: women that love
Are most uncertain, and one minute crave,
What in another they refuse to have. [*Exit.*

Scena Quinta.

Enter Clodio, Charino.

Clo. Assure thy self *Charino,* I am alter'd
From what I was; the tempests we have met with
In our uncertain voyage, were smooth gales
Compar'd to those, the memory of my lusts
Rais'd in my Conscience: and if ere again

I live to see *Zenocia*, I will sue,
And seek to her as a Lover, and a Servant,
And not command affection, like a Tyrant.

Char. In hearing this, you make me young again,
And Heaven, it seems, favouring this good change in you
In setting of a period to our dangers
Gives us fair hopes to find that here in *Lisbon*
Which hitherto in vain we long have sought for.
I have receiv'd assur'd intelligence,
Such strangers have been seen here: and though yet
I cannot learn their fortunes, nor the place
Of their abode, I have a Soul presages
A fortunate event here.

Clo. There have pass'd
A mutual enterchange of courtesies
Between me, and the Governour; therefore boldly
We may presume of him, and of his power
If we finde cause to use them, otherwise
I would not be known here, and these disguises
Will keep us from discovery.

Enter Manuel, Doctor, Arnoldo, Guard.

Char. What are these?

Clo. The Governour: with him my Rival, bound.

Char. For certain 'tis *Arnoldo.*

Clo. Let's attend What the success will be.

Mar. Is't possible There should be hope of his recovery, His wounds so many and so deadly?

Doct. So they appear'd at first, but the blood stop'd, His trance forsook him, and on better search We found they were not mortal.

Man. Use all care
To perfect this unhop'd for cure: that done

Propose your own rewards: and till you shall
Hear farther from me, for some ends I have,
Conceal it from his Mother.

Doct. Wee'l not fail Sir. [*Exit.*

Man. You still stand confident on your innocence.

Arn. It is my best and last guard, which I will not Leave, to relye on your uncertain mercy.

Enter Hippolyta, Zabulon, Leopold, Zenocia, 2 Servants.

Hip. Who bad you follow me! Goe home, and you Sir, As you respect me, goe with her.

Arn. Zenocia! And in her house a Servant!

Char. 'Tis my Daughter.

Clo. My love? Contain your joy, observe the sequel. [*Zen. passes.*

Man. Fye Madam, how undecent 'tis for you,
So far unlike your self to bee seen thus
In th' open streets? why do you kneel? pray you rise,
I am acquainted with the wrong, and loss
You have sustain'd, and the Delinquent now
Stands ready for his punishment.

Hip. Let it fall, Sir,
On the offender: he is innocent,
And most unworthy of these bonds he wears,
But I made up of guilt.

Man. What strange turn's this?

Leo. This was my prisoner once.

Hip. If chastity
In a young man, and tempted to the height too
Did ere deserve reward, or admiration,
He justly may claim both. Love to his person
(Or if you please give it a fouler name)

Compel'd me first to train him to my house,
All engines I rais'd there to shake his vertue,
Which in the assault were useless; he unmov'd still
As if he had no part of humane frailty.
Against the nature of my Sex, almost
I plaid the Ravisher. You might have seen
In our contention, young *Apollo* fly
And love-sick *Daphne* follow, all arts failing,
By flight he wan the victory, breaking from
My scorn'd embraces: the repulse (in women
Unsufferable) invited me to practise
A means to be reveng'd: and from this grew
His Accusation, and the abuse
Of your still equall justice: My rage ever
Thanks heaven, though wanton, I found not my self
So far engag'd to Hell, to prosecute
To the death what I had plotted, for that love
That made me first desire him, then accuse him,
Commands me with the hazard of my self
First to entreat his pardon, then acquit him.

Man. What ere you are, so much I love your vertue,
That I desire your friendship: do you unloose him
From those bonds, you are worthy of: your repentance
Makes part of satisfaction; yet I must
Severely reprehend you.

Leo. I am made A stale on all parts: But this fellow shall Pay dearly for her favour.

Arn. My life's so full
Of various changes, that I now despair
Of any certain port; one trouble ending,
A new, and worse succeeds it: what should *Zenocia*
Do in this womans house? Can chastity
And hot Lust dwell together without infection?
I would not be or jealous, or secure,
Yet something must be done, to sound the depth on't:

That she lives is my bliss, but living there,
A hell of torments; there's no way to her
In whom I live, but by this door, through which
To me 'tis death to enter, yet I must,
And will make tryal.

Man. Let me hear no more
Of these devices, Lady: this I pardon,
And at your intercession I forgive
Your instrument the Jew too: get you home.
The hundred thousand crowns you lent the City
Towards the setting forth of the last Navy
Bound for the Islands, was a good then, which
I ballance with your ill now.

Char. Now Sir, to him, You know my Daughter needs it.

Hip. Let me take
A farewell with mine eye, Sir, though my lip
Be barr'd the Ceremonie, courtesie
And Custom too allows of.

Arn. Gentle Madam,
I neither am so cold, nor so ill bred
But that I dare receive it: you are unguarded,
And let me tell you that I am asham'd
Of my late rudeness, and would gladly therefore
If you please to accept my ready service
Wait on you to your house.

Hip. Above my hope: Sir, if an Angel were to be my convoy, He should not be more welcom. – [*Ex.* Arn. *and* Hip.

Clo. Now you know me.

Man. Yes Sir, and honour you: ever remembring
Your many bounties, being ambitious only
To give you cause to say by some one service

That I am not ungratefull.

Clod. 'Tis now offer'd: I have a suit to you, and an easie one, Which e're long you shall know.

Man. When you think fit Sir,
And then as a command I will receive it,
Till when, most welcom: you are welcom too Sir,
'Tis spoken from the heart, and therefore needs not
Much protestation: at your better leisure
I will enquire the cause that brought you hither:
In the mean time serve you.

Clod. You out-doe me Sir. [*Exeunt.*

Actus Quartus. Scena Prima.

Enter Duarte, Doctor.

Dua. You have bestow'd on me a second life,
For which I live your creature, and have better'd
What nature fram'd unperfect, my first being
Insolent pride made monstrous; but this later
In learning me to know my self, hath taught me
Not to wrong others.

Doct. Then we live indeed,
When we can goe to rest without alarm
Given every minute to a guilt-sick conscience
To keep us waking, and rise in the morning
Secure in being innocent: but when
In the remembrance of our worser actions
We ever bear about us whips and furies,
To make the day a night of sorrow to us,

Even life's a burthen.

Dua. I have found and felt it;
But will endeavour having first made peace
With those intestine enemies my rude passions,
To be so with man-kind: but worthy Doctor,
Pray if you can resolve me; was the Gentleman
That left me dead, ere brought unto his tryal?

Doct. Not known, nor apprehended.

Dua. That's my grief.

Doct. Why, do you wish he had been punished?

Dua. No,
The stream of my swoln sorrow runs not that way:
For could I find him, as I vow to Heaven
It shall be my first care to seek him out,
I would with thanks acknowledge that his sword,
In opening my veins, which proud bloud poison'd,
Gave the first symptoms of true health.

Doct. 'Tis in you
A Christian resolution: that you live
Is by the Governours, your Uncles charge
As yet conceal'd. And though a sons loss never
Was solemniz'd with more tears of true sorrow
Than have been paid by your unequal'd Mother
For your supposed death, she's not acquainted
With your recovery.

Dua. For some few dayes Pray let her so continue: thus disguis'd I may abroad unknown.

Doct. Without suspicion Of being discovered.

Dua. I am confident
No moisture sooner dies than womens tears,
And therefore though I know my Mother vertuous,

Yet being one of that frail sex I purpose
Her farther tryal.

Doct. That as you think fit—I'le not betray you.

Dua. To find out this stranger
This true Physician of my mind and manners
Were such a blessing. He seem'd poor, and may
Perhaps be now in want; would I could find him.
The Innes I'le search first, then the publick Stewes;
He was of *Italy*, and that Country breeds not
Precisians that way, but hot Libertines;
And such the most are: 'tis but a little travail:
I am unfurnisht too, pray Mr. Doctor,
Can you supply me?

Doct. With what summ you please.

Dua. I will not be long absent.

Doct. That I wish too; For till you have more strength, I would not have you To be too bold.

Dua. Fear not, I will be carefull. [*Exeunt.*

Enter Leopold, Zabulon, Bravo.

Zab. I have brought him Sir, a fellow that will do it Though Hell stood in his way, ever provided You pay him for't.

Leop. He has a strange aspect, And looks much like the figure of a hang-man In a table of the Passion.

Zab. He transcends
All precedents, believe it, a flesh'd ruffian,
That hath so often taken the Strappado,
That 'tis to him but as a lofty trick
Is to a tumbler: he hath perused too
All Dungeons in *Portu[g]al*, thrice seven years
Rowed in the Galleys for three several murthers,
Though I presume that he has done a hundred,

And scap't unpunisht.

Leop. He is much in debt to you, You set him off so well. What will you take Sir To beat a fellow for me, that thus wrong'd me?

Bra. To beat him say you?

Leop. Yes, beat him to lameness, To cut his lips or nose off; any thing, That may disfigure him.

Bra. Let me consider? Five hundred pistolets for such a service I think were no dear penniworth.

Zab. Five hundred! Why there are of your Brother-hood in the City, I'le undertake, shall kill a man for twenty.

Bra. Kill him? I think so; I'le kill any man For half the mony.

Leop. And will you ask more For a sound beating than a murther?

Bra. I Sir,
And with good reason, for a dog that's dead,
The Spanish proverb says, will never bite:
But should I beat or hurt him only, he may
Recover, and kill me.

Leo. A good conclusion,
The obduracie of this rascal makes me tender.
I'le run some other course, there's your reward
Without the employment.

Bra. For that as you please Sir; When you have need to kill a man, pray use me, But I am out at beating. [*Exit.*

Zab. What's to be done then?

Leop. I'le tell thee *Zabulon*, and make thee privy To my most near designs: this stranger, which *Hippolyta* so dotes on, was my prisoner When the last Virgin, I bestowed upon her, Was made my prize; how he escaped, hereafter I'le let thee know; and it may be the love He bears the servant, makes him scorn the Mistris.

Zab. 'Tis not unlike; for the first time he saw her
His looks exprest so much, and for more proof
Since he came to my Ladys house, though yet
He never knew her, he hath practis'd with me
To help him to a conference, without
The knowledge of *Hippolyta;* which I promis'd.

Leop. And by all means perform it for their meeting,
But work it so, that my disdainful Mistris
(Whom, notwithstanding all her injuries,
'Tis my hard fate to love) may see and hear them.

Zab. To what end Sir?

Leop. This *Zabulon*: when she sees
Who is her rival, and her Lovers baseness
To leave a Princess for her bondwoman,
The sight will make her scorn, what now she dotes on,
I'le double thy reward.

Zab. You are like to speed then:
For I confess what you will soon believe,
We serve them best that are most apt to give,
For you, I'le place you where you shall see all, and yet be unobser-
v'd.

Leop. That I desire too. [*Exeunt.*

Enter Arnoldo.

Arn. I cannot see her yet, how it afflicts me
The poyson of this place should mix it self
With her pure thoughts? 'Twas she that was commanded,
Or my eyes failed me grosly; that youth, that face
And all that noble sweetness. May she not live here,
And yet be honest still?

Enter Zenocia.

Zen. It is *Arnoldo,*
From all his dangers free; fortune I bless thee.
My noble husband! how my joy swells in me,
But why in this place? what business hath he here?
He cannot hear of me, I am not known here.
I left him vertuous; how I shake to think now!
And how that joy I had, cools, and forsakes me!

Enter above Hippolyta *and* Zabulon.

This Lady is but fair, I have been thought so
Without compare admired; She has bewitched him
And he forgot—

Arn. 'Tis she again, the same—the same *Zenocia.*

Zab. There they are together.—Now you may mark.

Hip. Peace, let 'em parly.

Arn. That you are well *Zenocia,* and once more Bless my despairing eyes, with your wisht presence, I thank the gods; but that I meet you here—

Hip. They are acquainted.

Zab. I found that secret Madam, When you co[m]manded her go home: pray hear 'em.

Zen. That you meet me here, ne're blush at that *Arnoldo.*
Your coming comes too late: I am a woman,
And one woman with another may be trusted;
Do you fear the house?

Arn. More than a fear, I know it, Know it not good, not honest.

Zen. What do you here then?
I'th' name of vertue why do you approach it?
Will you confess the doubt and yet pursue it?
Where have your eyes been wandring, my *Arnoldo*?
What constancy, what faith do you call this? Fie,
Aim at one wanton mark, and wound another?

I do confess, the Lady fair, most beauteous,
And able to betray a strong mans liberty,
[Leopold *places himself unseen below.*
But you that have a love, a wife—you do well
To deal thus wisely with me: yet *Arnoldo,*
Since you are pleas'd to study a new beauty,
And think this old and ill, beaten with misery,
Study a nobler way for shame to love me,
Wrong not her honesty.

Arn. You have confirm'd me.

Zen. Who though she be your wife, will never hinder you,
So much I rest a servant to your wishes,
And love your Loves, though they be my destructions,
No man shall know me, nor the share I have in thee,
No eye suspect I am able to prevent you,
For since I am a slave to this great Lady,
Whom I perceive you follow,

Arn. Be not blinded.

Zen. Fortune shall make me useful to your service, I will speak for you.

Arn. Speak for me? you wrong me.

Zen. I will endeavour all the wayes I am able
To make her think well of you; will that please?
To make her dote upon you, dote to madness,
So far against my self I will obey you.
But when that's done, and I have shewed this duty,
This great obedience, few will buy it at my price,
Thus will I shake hands with you, wish you well,
But never see you more, nor receive comfort
From any thing, *Arnoldo.*

Arn. You are too tender;
I neither doubt you, nor desire longer
To be a man, and live, than I am honest

And only yours; our infinite affections
Abus'd us both.

Zab. Where are your favours now? The courtesies you shew'd this stranger, Madam?

Hip. Have I now found the cause?

Zab. Attend it further.

Zen. Did she invite you, do you say?

Arn. Most cunningly, And with a preparation of that state I was brought in and welcom'd.

Zen. Seem'd to love you?

Arn. Most infinitely, at first sight, most dotingly.

Zen. She is a goodly Lady.

Arn. Wondrous handsom:
At first view, being taken unprepar'd,
Your memory not present then to assist me,
She seem'd so glorious sweet, and so far stir'd me,
Nay be not jealous, there's no harm done.

Zen. Prethee—didst thou not kiss, *Arnoldo*?

Arn. Yes faith did I.

Zen. And then—

Arn. I durst not, did not—

Zen. I forgive you, Come tell the truth.

Arn. May be I lay with her.

Hip. He mocks me too, most basely.

Zen. Did ye faith? did ye forget so far?

Arn. Come, come, no weeping;
I would have lyen first in my grave, believe that.
Why will you ask those things you would not hear?
She is too untemperate to betray my vertues,

Too openly lascivious: had she dealt
But with that seeming modesty she might,
And flung a little Art upon her ardor,
But 'twas forgot, and I forgot to like her,
And glad I was deceiv'd. No my *Zenocia,*
My first love here begun, rests here unreapt yet,
And here for ever.

Zen. You have made me happy, Even in the midst of bondage blest.

Zab. You see now What rubs are in your way.

Hip. And quickly *Zabulon* I'le root 'em out.—Be sure you do this presently.

Zab. Do not you alter then.

Hip. I am resolute. [*Exit Zabulon.*

Arn. To see you only I came hither last, Drawn by no love of hers, nor base allurements, For by this holy light I hate her heartily.

Leop. I am glad of that, you have sav'd me so much vengeance And so much fear, From this hour fair befal you.

Arn. Some means I shall make shortly to redeem you, Till when, observe her well, and fit her temper, Only her lust contemn.

Zen. When shall I see you?

Arn. I will live hereabouts, and bear her fair still, Till I can find a fit hour to redeem you.

Hip. Shut all the doors.

Arn. Who's that?

Zen. We are betray'd, The Lady of the house has heard our parly, Seen us, and seen our Loves.

Hip. You courteous Gallant,
You that scorn all I can bestow, that laugh at
The afflictions, and the groans I suffer for you,
That slight and jeer my love, contemn the fortune
My favours can fling on you, have I caught you?

Have I now found the cause? ye fool my wishes;
Is mine own slave, my bane? I nourish that
That sucks up my content. I'le pray no more,
Nor wooe no more; thou shalt see foolish man,
And to thy bitter pain and anguish, look on
The vengeance I shall take, provok'd and slighted;
Redeem her then, and steal her hence: ho *Zabulon*
Now to your work.

Enter Zabulon, *and* Servants, *some holding* Arnoldo, *some ready with a cord to strangle* Zenocia.

Arn. Lady, but hear me speak first, As you have pity.

Hip. I have none. You taught me, When I even hung about your neck, you scorn'd me.

Zab. Shall we pluck yet?

Hip. No, hold a little *Zabulon,* I'le pluck his heart-strings first: now am I worthy A little of your love?

Arn. I'le be your Servant, Command me through what danger you shall aime at, Let it be death.

Hip. Be sure Sir, I shall fit you.

Arn. But spare this Virgin.

Hip. I would spare that villain first, Had cut my Fathers throat.

Arn. Bounteous Lady, If in your sex there be that noble softness, That tenderness of heart, women are crown'd for—

Zen. Kneel not *Arnoldo*, doe her not that honour,
She is not worthy such submission,
I scorn a life depends upon her pity.
Proud woman do thy worst, and arm thy anger
With thoughts as black as Hell, as hot and bloody,
I bring a patience here, shall make 'em blush,
An innocence, shall outlook thee, and death too.

Arn. Make me your slave, I give my freedom to ye,
For ever to be fetter'd to your service;

'Twas I offended, be not so unjust then,
To strike the innocent, this gentle maid
Never intended fear and doubt against you:
She is your Servant, pay not her observance
With cruel looks, her duteous faith with death.

Hip. Am I fair now? now am I worth your liking?

Zen. Not fair, not to be liked, thou glorious Devil, Thou vernisht piece of lust, thou painted fury.

Arn. Speak gently sweet, speak gently.

Zen. I'le speak nobly.
'Tis not the saving of a life I aim at,
Mark me lascivious woman, mark me truly,
And then consider, how I weigh thy anger.
Life is no longer mine, nor dear unto me,
Than usefull to his honour I preserve it.
If thou hadst studied all the courtesies
Humanity and noble blood are linkt to,
Thou couldst not have propounded such a benefit,
Nor heapt upon me such unlookt for honour
As dying for his sake, to be his Martyr,
'Tis such a grace.

Hip. You shall not want that favour, Let your bones work miracles.

Arn. Dear Lady By those fair eyes—

Hip. There is but this way left ye To save her life.—

Arn. Speak it, and I embrace it.

Hip. Come to my private chamber presently, And there, what love and I command—

Arn. I'le doe it, Be comforted *Zenocia.*

Zen. Do not do this
To save me, do not lose your self I charge you,
I charge you by your love, that love [you] bear me;

That love, that constant love you have twin'd to me,
By all your promises, take heed you keep 'em,
Now is your constant tryal. If thou dost this,
Or mov'st one foot, to guide thee to her lust,
My curses and eternal hate pursue thee.
Redeem me at the base price of dis-loyalty?
Must my undoubted honesty be thy Bawd too?
Go and intwine thy self about that body;
Tell her, for my life thou hast lost thine honour,
Pull'd all thy vows from heaven, basely, most basely
Stoop'd to the servile flames of that foul woman,
To add an hour to me that hate thee for it,
Know thee not again, nor name thee for a Husband.

Arn. What shall I do to save her?

Hip. How now, what hast there?

Enter a Servant.

Ser. The Governour, attended with some Gentlemen, Are newly entred, to speak with your Ladiship.

Hip. Pox o' their business, reprieve her for this hour, I shall have other time.

Arn. Now fortune help us.

Hip. I'le meet 'em presently: retire awhile all. [*Exeunt.*

Zab. You rise to day upon your right side Lady;
You know the danger too, and may prevent it,
And if you suffer her to perish thus,
As she must do, and suddenly, believe it,
Unless you stand her friend; you know the way on't,
I guess you poorly love her, less your fortune.
Let her know nothing, and perform this matter,
There are hours ordained for several businesses,
You understand.

Arn. I understand you Bawd Sir, And such a Counsellour I never car'd for.

Enter the Governour, Clodio, Leopold, Charino *and* Attendants *at one door*, Hippolyta *at the other.*

Hip. Your Lordship does me honour.

Gover. Fair *Hippolyta*, I am come to ease you of a charge.

Hip. I keep none I count a burthen Sir: and yet I lye too.

Gover. Which is the Maid; is she here?

Clod. Yes Sir, This is she, this is *Zenocia*, The very same I sued to your Lordship for.

Zen. Clodio again? more misery? more ruin? Under what angry star is my life govern'd?

Gov. Come hither Maid, you are once more a free woman, Here I discharge your bonds.

Arn. Another smile, Another trick of fortune to betray us!

Hip. Why does your Lordship use me so unnobly? Against my will to take away my bond-woman?

Gov. She was no lawful prize, therefore no bond-woman:
She's of that Country we hold friendship with,
And ever did, and therefore to be used
With entertainment, fair and courteous.
The breach of League in us gives foul example,
Therefore you must be pleas'd to think this honest;
Did you know what she was?

Leop. Not till this instant; For had I known her, she had been no prisoner.

Gov. There, take the Maid, she is at her own dispose now, And if there be ought else to do your honour Any poor service in—

Clod. I am vowed your servant.

Arn. Your Father's here too, that's our only comfort, And in a Country now, we stand free people, Where *Clodio* has no power, be comforted.

Zen. I fear some trick yet.

Arn. Be not so dejected.

Gover. You must not be displeas'd; so farewel Lady. Come Gentlemen; Captain, you must with me too, I have a little business.

Leop. I attend your Lordship: Now my way's free, and my hope's Lord again. [*Exeunt all but* Hip. *and* Zab.

Hip. D'ye jeer me now ye are going? I may live yet—to make you howl both.

Zab. You might have done; you had power then,
But now the chains are off, the command lost,
And such a story they will make of this
To laugh out lazie time.

Hip. No means yet left me? For now I burst with anger: none to satisfie me? No comfort? no revenge?

Zab. You speak too late;
You might have had all these, your useful servants,
Had you been wise, and suddain: what power, or will
Over her beauty, have you now? by violence
To constrain his love; she is as free as you are,
And no law can impeach her liberty,
And whilst she is so, *Arnoldo* will despise you.

Hip. Either my love or anger must be satisfied, Or I must dye.

Zab. I have a way wou'd do it, Wou'd do it yet, protect me from the Law.

Hip. From any thing; thou knowest what power I have, What mony, and what friends.

Zab. 'Tis a devilish one: But such must now be us'd: walk in, I'le tell you; And if you like it, if the Devil can do any thing—

Hip. Devil, or what thou wilt, so I be satisfied. [*Ex.*

Enter Sulpitia, *and* Jaques.

Sulp. This is the rarest and the lustiest fellow, And so bestirs himself—

Jaq. Give him breath Mistress, You'l melt him else.

Sulp. He does perform such wonders— The women are mad on him.

Jaq. Give him breath I say; The man is but a man, he must have breath.

Sulp. How many had he yesterday? And they paid bravely too.

Jaq. About fourteen, But still I cry give breath, spare him and have him.

Sulp. Five Dames to day; this was a small stage, He may endure five more.

Jaq. Breath, breath I cry still; Body o' me give breath, the man's a lost man else. Feed him and give him breath.

Enter 2 Gentlewomen.

Sulp. Welcome Gentlewomen, Y'are very welcome.

1 Gen. We hear you have a lusty and well complexion'd fellow That does rare tricks; my Sister and my self here, Would trifle out an hour or two, so please you.

Sulp. Jaques, conduct 'em in.

Both. There's for your courtesie. [*Ex.* Jaq. *and* Gent.

Sulp. Good pay still, good round pay, this happy fellow
Will set me up again; he brings in gold
Faster than I have leisure to receive it.
O that his body were not flesh and fading;
But I'le so pap him up—nothing too dear for him;
What a sweet scent he has?—Now what news *Jaques*?

Jaq. He cannot last, I pity the poor man,
I suffer for him; two Coaches of young City dames,
And they drive as the Devil were in the wheels,
Are ready now to enter: and behind these
An old dead-palsied Lady in a Litter,
And she makes all the haste she can: the man's lost,
You may gather up his dry bones to make Nine-pins,

But for his flesh.

Sulp. These are but easie labours Yet, for I know he must have rest.

Ja. He must—you'll beat him off his legs else presently.

Sul. Go in, and bid him please himself, I am pleas'd too:
To morrow's a new day; but if he can
I would have him take pity o' the old Lady.
Alas 'tis charity.

Jaq. I'le tell him all this, And if he be not too fool-hardy.

Enter Zabulon.

Sulp. How now? What news with you?

Zab. You must presently Shew all the art you have, and for my Lady.

Sulp. She may command.

Zab. You must not dream nor trifle.

Sulp. Which way?

Zab. A spell you must prepare, a powerful one,
Peruse but these directions, you shall find all;
There is the picture too, be quick, and faithful,
And do it with that strength—when 'tis perform'd,
Pitch your reward at what you please, you have it.

Sul. I'le do my best, and suddenly: but hark ye, Will you never lye at home again?

Zab. Excuse me, I have too much business yet.

Sulp. I am right glad on't.

Zab. Think on your business, so farewel.

Sulp. I'le do it.

Zab. Within this hour I'le visit you again And give you greater lights.

Sulp. I shall observe ye; This brings a brave reward, bravely I'le do it, And all the hidden art I have, express in't. [*Exeunt at both doors.*

Enter Rutilio *with a Night-cap.*

Rut. Now do I look as if I were Crow-trodden,
Fye, how my hams shrink under me! O me,
I am broken-winded too; is this a life?
Is this the recreation I have aim'd at?
I had a body once, a handsome body,
And wholesome too. Now I appear like a rascal,
That had been hung a year or two in Gibbets.
Fye how I faint! women? keep me from women;
Place me before a Cannon, 'tis a pleasure;
Stretch me upon a Rack, a recreation;
But women? women? O the Devil! women?
Curtius Gulf was never half so dangerous.
Is there no way to find the Trap-door again,
And fall into the Cellar, and be taken?
No lucky fortune to direct me that way?
No Gallies to be got, nor yet no Gallows?
For I fear nothing now, no earthly thing
But these unsatisfied Men-leeches, women.
How devilishly my bones ake! O the old Lady!
I have a kind of waiting-woman lyes cross my back too,
O how she stings! no treason to deliver me?
Now what are you? do you mock me?

Enter 3. *with Night-caps very faintly.*

1 No Sir, no; We were your Predecessors in this place.

2 And come to see you bear up.

Rut. Good Gentlemen; You seem to have a snuffing in your head Sir, A parlous snuffing, but this same dampish air—

2 A dampish air indeed.

Rut. Blow your face tenderly,
Your nose will ne're endure it: mercy o' me,
What are men chang'd to here? is my nose fast yet?

Me thinks it shakes i'th' hilts: pray tell me gentlemen,
How long is't since you flourisht here?

3 Not long since.

Rut. Move your self easily, I see you are tender, Nor long endured.

2 The labour was so much Sir, And so few to perform it—

Rut. Must I come to this?
And draw my legs after me like a lame Dog?
I cannot run away, I am too feeble:
Will you sue for this place again Gentlemen?

1 No truly Sir, the place has been too warm for our complexions.
We have enough on't, rest you merry Sir,
We came but to congratulate your fortune,
You have abundance.

3 Bear your fortune soberly, And so we leave you to the next fair Lady. [*Ex. the* 3.

Rut. Stay but a little, and I'le meet you Gentlemen,
At the next Hospital: there's no living thus,
Nor am I able to endure it longer,
With all the helps and heats that can be given me,
I am at my trot already: they are fair and young
Most of the women that repair unto me,
But they stick on like Burs, shake me like Feathers.

Enter Sulpitia.

More Women yet?
Would I were honestly married
To any thing that had but half a face,
And not a groat to keep her, nor a smock,
That I might be civilly merry when I pleased,
Rather than labouring in these Fulling-mills.

Sul. By this the spell begins to work: you are lusty, I see you bear up bravely yet.

Rut. Do you hear Lady,
Do not make a game-bear of me, to play me hourly,
And fling on all your whelps; it would not hold;
Play me with some discretion; to day one course,
And two dayes hence another.

Sulp. If you be so angry
Pay back the mony I redeem'd you at
And take your course, I can have men enough:
You have cost me a hundred crowns since you came hither,
In Broths and strength[n]ing Caudles; till you do pay me,
If you will eat and live, you shall endeavour,
I'le chain you to't else.

Rut. Make me a Dog-kennel,
I'le keep your house and bark, and feed on bare bones,
And be whipt out o' doors,
Do you mark me Lady? whipt,
I'le eat old shoes.

Enter Duarte.

Dua. In this house I am told
There is a stranger, of a goodly person,
And such a one there was; if I could see him,
I yet remember him.

Sulp. Your business Sir, If it be for a woman, ye are couzen'd, I keep none here. [*Exit.*

Dua. Certain this is the Gentleman; The very same.

Rut. Death, if I had but mony,
Or any friend to bring me from this bondage,
I would Thresh, set up a Cobler's shop, keep Hogs,
And feed with 'em, sell Tinder-boxes,

And Knights of Ginger-bread, Thatch for three
Half pence a day, and think it Lordly,
From this base Stallion trade: why does he eye me,
Eye me so narrowly?

Dua. It seems you are troubled Sir, I heard you speak of want.

Rut. 'Tis better hearing Far, than relieving Sir.

Dua. I do not think so, you know me not.

Rut. Not yet that I remember.

Dua. You shall, and for your friend: I am beholding to ye,
Greatly beholding Sir; if you remember,
You fought with such a man, they call'd *Duarte,*
A proud distemper'd man: he was my enemy,
My mortal foe, you slew him fairly, nobly.

Rut. Speak softly Sir, you do not mean to betray me, I wisht the Gallows, now th'are coming fairly.

Dua. Be confident, for as I live, I love you,
And now you shall perceive it: for that service,
Me, and my purse command: there, take it to ye,
'Tis gold, and no small sum, a thousand Duckets,
Supply your want.

Rut. But do you do this faithfully?

Dua. If I mean ill, spit in my face and kick me: In what else I may serve you, Sir—

Rut. I thank you,
This is as strange to me as Knights adventures.
I have a project, 'tis an honest one,
And now I'le tempt my fortune.

Dua. Trust me with it.

Rut. You are so good and honest I must trust ye, 'Tis but to carry a letter to a Lady That sav'd my life once.

Dua. That will be most thankful, I will do't with all care.

Rut. Where are you, white-broth?
Now lusty blood,
Come in, and tell your mony:
'Tis ready here, no threats, nor no orations,
Nor prayers now.

Sulp. You do not mean to leave me.

Rut. I'le live in Hell sooner than here, and cooler. Come quickly come, dispatch, this air's unwho[l]som: Quickly good Lady, quickly to't.

Sulp. Well, since it must be, The next I'le fetter faster sure, and closer.

Rut. And pick his bones, as y'have done mine, pox take ye.

Dua. At my lodging for a while, you shall be quartered, And there take Physick for your health.

Rut. I thank ye, I have found my angel now too, if I can keep him. [*Exeunt omnes.*

Actus Quintus. Scena Prima.

Enter Rutilio and Duarte.

_Rut. You like the Letter?

Dua. Yes, but I must tell you
You tempt a desperate hazard, to sollicite
The mother, (and the grieved one too, 'tis rumor'd)
Of him you slew so lately.

Rut. I have told you
Some proofs of her affection, and I know not

A nearer way to make her satisfaction
For a lost Son, than speedily to help her
To a good Husband; one that will beget
Both Sons and Daughters, if she be not barren.
I have had a breathing now, and have recovered
What I lost in my late service, 'twas a hot one:
It fired and fired me; but all thanks to you Sir,
You have both freed and cool'd me.

Dua. What is done Sir, I thought well done, and was in that rewarded, And therefore spare your thanks.

Rut. I'le no more Whoring:
This fencing 'twixt a pair of sheets, more wears one
Than all the exercise in the world besides.
To be drunk with good Canary, a meer Julip
Or like gourd-water to't; twenty Surfeits
Come short of one nights work there. If I get this Lady
As ten to one I shall, I was ne're denied yet,
I will live wondrous honestly; walk before her
Gravely and demurely
And then instruct my family; you are sad,
What do you muse on Sir?

Dua. Truth I was thinking
What course to take for the delivery of your letter,
And now I have it: but faith did this Lady
(For do not gull your self) for certain know,
You kill'd her Son?

Rut. Give me a Book I'le swear't;
Denyed me to the Officers, that pursued me,
Brought me her self to th' door, then gave me gold
To bear my charges, and shall I make doubt then
But that she lov'd me? I am confident
Time having ta'ne her grief off, that I shall be
Most welcome to her: for then to have wooed her

Had been unseasonable.

Dua. Well Sir, there's more mony, To ma[ke] you handsome; I'le about your business: You know where you must stay?

Rut. There you shall find me:
Would I could meet my Brother now, to know,
Whether the Jew, his Genius, or my Christian,
Has prov'd the better friend. [*Exit.*

Dua. O who would trust
Deceiving woman! or believe that one
The best, and most Canoniz'd ever was
More than a seeming goodness? I could rail now
Against the sex, and curse it; but the theam
And way's too common: yet that *Guiomar*
My Mother; (nor let that forbid her to be
The wonder of our nation) she that was
Mark'd out the great example, for all Matrons
Both Wife and Widow; she that in my breeding
Exprest the utmost of a Mothers care,
And tenderness to a Son; she that yet feigns
Such sorrow for me; good God, that this mother,
After all this, should give up to a stranger,
The wreak she ow'd her Son; I fear her honour.
That he was sav'd, much joyes me, and grieve only
That she was his preserver. I'le try further,
And by this Engine, find whether the tears,
Of which she is so prodigal, are for me,
Or us'd to cloak her base hypocrisie. [*Exit.*

Enter Hippolyta *and* Sulpitia.

Hip. Are you assur'd the charm prevails?

Sulp. Do I live?
Or do you speak to me? Now this very instant
Health takes its last leave of her; meager paleness
Like winter, nips the Roses and the Lilies,

The Spring that youth, and love adorn'd her face with.
To force affection, is beyond our art,
For I have prov'd all means that hell has taught me,
Or the malice of a woman, which exceeds it,
To change *Arnoldo's* love, but to no purpose:
But for your bond-woman—

Hip. Let her pine and dye;
She remov'd, which like a brighter Sun,
Obscures my beams, I may shine out again,
And as I have been, be admir'd and sought to:
How long has she to live?

Sulp. Lady, before
The Sun twice rise and set, be confident,
She is but dead; I know my Charm hath found her.
Nor can the Governours Guard; her lovers tears;
Her Fathers sorrow, or his power that freed her,
Defend her from it.

Enter Zabulon.

Zab. All things have succeeded,
As you could wish; I saw her brought sick home;
The image of pale death, stampt on her fore-head.
Let me adore this second Hecate,
This great Commandress, of the fatal Sisters,
That as she pleases, can cut short, or lengthen
The thread of life.

Hip. Where was she when the inchantment First seis'd upon her?

Zab. Taking the fresh air,
In the company of the Governour, and Count *Clodio,*
Arnoldo too, was present with her Father,
When, in a moment (so the servants told me)
As she was giving thanks to the Governour,
And *Clodio,* for her unexpected freedom,

As if she had been blasted, she sunk down,
To their amazement.

Hip. 'Tis thy master-piece
Which I will so reward, that thou shalt fix here,
And with the hazard of thy life, no more
Make tryal of thy powerful Art; which known
Our Laws call death: off with this Magical Robe,
And be thy self.

Enter Governour, Clodio, *and* Charino.

Sulp. Stand close, you shall hear more.

Man. You must have patience; all rage is vain now,
And piety forbids, that we should question
What is decreed above, or ask a reason
Why heaven determines this or that way of us.

Clod. Heaven has no hand in't; 'tis a work of hell.
Her life hath been so innocent, all her actions
So free from the suspicion of crime,
As rather she deserves a Saints place here,
Than to endure, what now her sweetness suffers.

Char. Not for her fault, but mine Sir, *Zenocia* suffers: The sin I made, when I sought to rase down *Arnoldo's* love, built on a Rock of truth, Now to the height is punish'd. I profess, Had he no birth, nor parts, the present sorrow He now expresses for her, does deserve her Above all Kings, though such had been his rivals.

Clod. All ancient stories, of the love of Husbands To vertuous Wives, be now no more remembred.

Char. The tales of *Turtles*, ever be forgotten, Or, for his sake believ'd.

Man. I have heard, there has been
Between some married pairs, such sympathy,
That th' Husband has felt really the throws

His Wife then teeming suffers, this true grief
Confirms, 'tis not impossible.

Clod. We shall find Fit time for this hereafter; let's use now All possible means to help her.

Man. Care, nor cost, Nor what Physicians can do, shall be wanting; Make use of any means or men.

Char. You are noble. [*Exeunt* Man. Clod, *and* Char.

Sulp. Ten Colledges of Doctors shall not save her. Her fate is in your hand.

Hip. Can I restore her?

Sulp. If you command my Art.

Hip. I'le dye my self first.
And yet I'le go visit her, and see
This miracle of sorrow in *Arnoldo*:
And 'twere for me, I should change places with her,
And dye most happy, such a lovers tears
Were a rich monument, but too good for her,
Whose misery I glory in: come *Sulpitia,*
You shall along with me, good *Zabulon*
Be not far off.

Zab. I will attend you Madam. [*Exeunt.*

Enter Duarte, *and a* Servant.

Ser. I have serv'd you from my youth, and ever
You have found me faithful: that you live's a treasure
I'le lock up here; nor shall it be let forth,
But when you give me warrant.

Dua. I rely
Upon thy faith; nay, no more protestations,
Too many of them will call that in question,
Which now I doubt not: she is there?

Ser. Alone too,
But take it on my life, your entertainment,
Appearing as you are, will be but course,
For the displeasure I shall undergo
I am prepar'd.

Dua. Leave me, I'le stand the hazard. [*Exit* Servant.
The silence that's observ'd, her close retirements,
No visitants admitted, not the day;
These sable colours, all signs of true sorrow,
Or hers is deeply counterfeit. I'le look nearer,
Manners give leave—she sits upon the ground;
By heaven she weeps; my picture in her hand too;
She kisses it and weeps again.

Enter Guiomar.

Gui. Who's there?

Dua. There is no starting back now Madam.

Gui. Ha, another murderer! I'le not protect thee, Though I have no more Sons.

Dua. Your pardon Lady, There's no such foul fact taints me.

Gui. What makes thou here then? Where are my servants, do none but my sorrows Attend upon me? speak, what brought thee hither?

Dua. A will to give you comfort.

Gui. Thou art but a man.
And 'tis beyond a humane reach to do it,
If thou could raise the dead out of their graves,
Bid time run back, make me now what I was,
A happy Mother; gladly I would hear thee,
But that's impossible.

Dua. Please you but read this; You shall know better there, why I am sent, Than if I should deliver it.

Gui. From whom comes it?

Dua. That will instruct you. I suspect this stranger,
Yet she spake something that holds such alliance
With his reports; I know not what to think on't;
What a frown was there? she looks me through, & through,
Now reads again, now pauses, and now smiles;
And yet there's more of anger in't than mirth,
These are strange changes; oh I understand it,
She's full of serious thoughts.

Gui. You are just, you Heavens,
And never do forget to hear their prayers,
That truly pay their vows, the defer'd vengeance,
For you, and my words sake so long defer'd,
Under which as a mountain my heart groans yet
When 'twas despair'd of, now is offer'd to me;
And if I lose it, I am both wayes guilty.
The womans mask, dissimulation help me.
Come hither friend, I am sure you know the Gentleman,
That sent these charms.

Dua. Charms Lady?

Gui. These charms;
I well may call them so, they've won upon me,
More than ere letter did; thou art his friend,
(The confidence he has in thee, confirms it)
And therefore I'le be open breasted to thee;
To hear of him, though yet I never saw him,
Was most desir'd of all men; let me blush,
And then I'le say I love him.

Dua. All men see, In this a womans vertue.

Gui. I expected
For the courtesie I did, long since to have seen him,
And though I then forbad it, you men know,
Between our hearts and tongues there's a large distance;

But I'le excuse him, may be hitherto
He has forborn it, in respect my Son
Fell by his hand.

Dua. And reason Lady.

Gui. No, he did me a pleasure in't, a riotous fellow,
And with that insolent, not worth the owning;
I have indeed kept a long solemn sorrow,
For my friends sake partly; but especially
For his long absence.

Dua. O the Devil.

Guio. Therefore
Bid him be speedy; a Priest shall be ready
To tye the holy knot; this kiss I send him,
Deliver that and bring him.

Dua. I am dumb: A good cause I have now, and a good sword, And something I shall do, I wait upon you. [*Exeunt.*

Enter Manuel, Charino, Arnoldo, Zenocia, *born in a chair*. 2 Doctors, Clodio.

Doct. Give her more air, she dyes else.

Arn. O thou dread power,
That mad'st this all, and of thy workmanship
This virgin wife, the Master piece, look down on her;
Let her minds virtues, cloth'd in this fair garment,
That worthily deserves a better name
Than flesh and bloud, now sue, and prevail for her.
Or if those are denyed, let innocence,
To which all passages in Heaven stand open,
Appear in her white robe, before thy throne;
And mediate for her: or if this age of sin
Be worthy of a miracle, the Sun
In his diurnal progress never saw

So sweet a subject to imploy it on.

Man. Wonders are ceas'd Sir, we must work by means.

Arno. 'Tis true, and such reverend Physicians are;
To you thus low I fall then; so may you ever
Be stil'd the hands of Heaven, natures restorers;
Get wealth and honours; and by your success,
In all your undertakings, propagate
Your great opinion in the world, as now
You use your saving art; for know good Gentlemen,
Besides the fame, and all that I possess,
For a reward, posterity shall stand
Indebted to you, for (as Heaven forbid it)
Should my *Zenocia* dye, robbing this age
Of all that's good or gracefull, times succeeding,
The story of her pure life not yet perfect,
Will suffer in the want of her example.

Doct. Were all the world to perish with her, we
Can do no more, than what art and experience
Give us assurance of, we have us'd all means
To find the cause of her disease, yet cannot;
How should we then, promise the cure?

Arn. Away,
I did bely you, when I charg'd you with
The power of doing, ye are meer names only,
And even your best perfection, accidental;
What ever malady thou art, or Spirit,
As some hold all diseases that afflict us,
As love already makes me sensible
Of half her sufferings, ease her of her part,
And let me stand the butt of thy fell malice,
And I will swear th'art mercifull.

Doct. Your hand Lady; What a strange heat is here! bring some warm water.

Arn. She shall use nothing that is yours; my sorrow Provides her of a better bath, my tears Shall do that office.

Zeno. O my best *Arnoldo*!
The truest of all lovers! I would live
Were heaven so pleas'd, but to reward your sorrow
With my true service; but since that's denied me,
May you live long and happy: do not suffer
(By your affection to me I conjure you)
My sickness to infect you; though much love
Makes you too subject to it.

Arn. In this only

Zenocia wrongs her servant; can the body
Subsist, the Soul departed? 'tis as easie
As I to live without you; I am your husband,
And long have been so, though our adverse fortune,
Bandying us from one hazard to another,
Would never grant me so much happiness,
As to pay a husbands debt; despite of fortune,
In death I'le follow you, and guard mine own;
And there enjoy what here my fate forbids me.

Clod. So true a sorrow, and so feelingly Exprest, I never read of.

Man. I am struck With wonder to behold it, as with pity.

Char. If you that are a stranger, suffer for them,
Being tied no further than humanity
Leads you to soft compassion; think great Sir,
What of necessity I must endure,
That am a Father?

Hippolyta, Zabulon, *and* Sulpitia *at the door.*

Zab. Wait me there, I hold it Unfit to have you seen; as I find cau-se, You shall proceed.

Man. You are welcom Lady.

Hip. Sir, I come to do a charitable office, How does the patient?

Clod. You may enquire
Of more than one; for two are sick, and deadly,
He languishes in her, her health's despair'd of,
And in hers, his.

Hip. 'Tis a strange spectacle, With what a patience they sit unmo-v'd! Are they not dead already?

Doct. By her pulse, She cannot last a day.

Arn. Oh by that summons, I know my time too!

Hip. Look to the man.

Clod. Apply
Your Art, to save the Lady, preserve her,
A town is your reward.

_Hip. I'le treble it, In ready gold, if you restore *Arnoldo*; For in his death I dye too.

Clod. Without her I am no more.

Arn. Are you there Madam? now
You may feast on my miseries; my coldness
In answering your affections, or hardness,
Give it what name you please, you are reveng'd of,
For now you may perceive, our thred of life
Was spun together, and the poor *Arnoldo*
Made only to enjoy the best *Zenocia,*
And not to serve the use of any other;
And in that she may equal; my Lord *Clodio*
Had long since else enjoyed her, nor could I
Have been so blind, as not to see your great
And many excellencies far, far beyond
Or my deservings, or my hopes; we are now
Going our latest journey, and together,
Our only comfort we desire, pray give it,

Your charity to our ashes, such we must be,
And not to curse our memories.

Hip. I am much mov'd.

Clod. I am wholly overcome, all love to women
Farewell for ever; ere you dye, your pardon;
And yours Sir; had she many years to live,
Perhaps I might look on her, as a Brother,
But as a lover never; and since all
Your sad misfortunes had original
From the barbarous Custom practis'd in my Country,
Heaven witness, for your sake I here release it;
So to your memory, chaste Wives and Virgins
Shall ever pay their vowes. I give her to you;
And wish, she were so now, as when my lust
Forc'd you to quit the Country.

Hip. It is in vain
To strive with destiny, here my dotage ends,
Look up *Zenocia*, health in me speaks to you;
She gives him to you, that by divers ways,
So long has kept him from you: and repent not,
That you were once my servant, for which health
In recompence of what I made you suffer,
The hundred thousand Crowns, the City owes me,
Shall be your dower.

Man. 'Tis a magnificent gift, Had it been timely given.

Hip. It is believe it, *Sulpitia.*

Enter a Servant, *and* Sulpitia.

Sulp. Madam.

Hip. Quick, undoe the charm; Ask not a reason why; let it suffice, It is my will.

Sulp. Which I obey and gladly. [*Exit.*

Man. Is to be married, sayest thou?

Ser. So she sayes Sir, And does desire your presence. [*They are born off in chairs.*

Man. And tell her I'le come.

Hip. Pray carry them to their rest; for though already, They do appear as dead, let my life pay for't, If they recover not.

Man. What you have warranted, Assure your self, will be expected from you; Look to them carefully; and till the tryal,—

Hip. Which shall not be above four hours.

Man. Let me
Intreat your companies: there is something
Of weight invites me hence.

All. We'll wait upon you. [*Exeunt.*

Enter Guiomar, *and* Servants.

Guio. You understand what my directions are, And what they guide you to; the faithfull promise You have made me all.

All. We do and will perform it.

Guio. The Governour will not fail to be here presently; Retire a while, till you shall find occasion, And bring me word, when they arrive.

All. Wee shall Madam.

Guio. Only stay you to entertain.

1 Ser. I am ready.

Guio. I wonder at the bold, and practis'd malice,
Men ever have o' foot against our honours,
That nothing we can do, never so vertuous,
No shape put on so pious, no not think
What a good is, be that good ne're so noble,
Never so laden with admir'd example,
But still we end in lust; our aims, our actions,
Nay, even our charities, with lust are branded;

Why should this stranger else, this wretched stranger,
Whose life I sav'd at what dear price sticks here yet,
Why should he hope? he was not here an hour,
And certainly in that time, I may swear it
I gave him no loose look, I had no reason;
Unless my tears were flames, my curses courtships;
The killing of my Son, a kindness to me.
Why should he send to me, or with what safety
(Examining the ruine he had wrought me)
Though at that time, my pious pity found him,
And my word fixt; I am troubled, strongly troubled.

Enter a Servant.

Ser. The Gentlemen are come.

Guio. Then bid 'em welcome—I must retire. [*Exit.*

Enter Rutilio, *and* Duarte.

Ser. You are welcom Gentlemen.

Rut. I thank you friend, I would speak with your Lady.

Ser. I'le let her understand.

Rut. It shall befit you. How do I look Sir, in this handsome trim? [*Exit* Servant. Me thinks I am wondrous brave.

Duar. You are very decent.

Rut. These by themselves, without more helps of nature,
Would set a woman hard; I know 'em all,
And where their first aims light; I'le lay my head on't,
I'le take her eye, as soon as she looks on me,
And if I come to speak once, woe be to her,
I have her in a nooze, she cannot scape me;
I have their several lasts.

Dua. You are throughly studied, But tell me Sir, being unacquainted with her, As you confess you are—

Rut. That's not an hours work, I'le make a Nun forget her beads in two hours.

Dua. She being set in years, next none of those lusters Appearing in her eye, that warm the fancy; Nor nothing in her face, but handsom ruines.

Rut. I love old stories: those live believ'd, Authentique,
When 20. of your modern faces are call'd in,
For new opinion, paintings, and corruptions;
Give me an old confirm'd face; besides she sav'd me,
She sav'd my life, have I not cause to love her?
She's rich and of a constant state, a fair one,
Have I not cause to wooe her? I have tryed sufficient
All your young Phillies, I think this back has try'd 'em,
And smarted for it too: they run away with me,
Take bitt between the teeth, and play the Devils;
A staied pace now becomes my years; a sure one,
Where I may sit and crack no girths.

Dua. How miserable,
If my Mother should confirm, what I suspect now,
Beyond all humane cure were my condition!
Then I shall wish, this body had been so too.
Here comes the Lady Sir.

Enter Guiomar.

Rut. Excellent Lady, To shew I am a creature, bound to your service, And only yours—

Guio. Keep at that distance Sir; For if you stir—

Rut. I am obedient.
She has found already, I am for her turn;
With what a greedy hawks eye she beholds me!
Mark how she musters all my parts.

Guio. A goodly Gentleman, Of a more manly set, I never look'd on.

Rut. Mark, mark her eyes still; mark but the carriage of 'em.

Guio. How happy am I now, since my Son fell,
He fell not by a base unnoble hand!
As that still troubled me; how far more happy
Shall my revenge be, since the Sacrifice,
I offer to his grave, shall be both worthy
A Sons untimely loss, and a Mothers sorrow!

Rut. Sir, I am made believe it; she is mine own,
I told you what a spell I carried with me,
All this time does she spend in contemplation
Of that unmatch'd delight: I shall be thankfull to ye;
And if you please to know my house, to use it;
To take it for your own.

Guio. Who waits without there?

Enter Guard, *and* Servants, *they seize upon* Rut. *and bind him.*

Rut. How now? what means this, Lady?

Guio. Bind him fast.

Rut. Are these the bride-laces you prepare for me? The colours that you give?

Dua. Fye Gentle Lady, This is not noble dealing.

Guio. Be you satisfied, I[t] seems you are a stranger to this meaning, You shall not be so long.

Rut. Do you call this wooing—Is there no end of womens persecutions?
Must I needs fool into mine own destruction?
Have I not had fair warnings, and enough too?
Still pick the Devils teeth? you are not mad Lady;
Do I come fairly, and like a Gentleman,
To offer you that honour?

Guio. You are deceiv'd Sir,
You come besotted, to your own destruction:
I sent not for you; what honour can ye add to me,

That brake that staff of honour, my age lean'd on?
That rob'd me of that right, made me a Mother?
Hear me thou wretched man, hear me with terrour,
And let thine own bold folly shake thy Soul,
Hear me pronounce thy death, that now hangs o're thee,
Thou desperate fool; who bad thee seek this ruine?
What mad unmanly fate, made thee discover
Thy cursed face to me again? was't not enough
To have the fair protection of my house,
When misery and justice close pursued thee?
When thine own bloudy sword, cryed out against thee,
Hatcht in the life of him? yet I forgave thee.
My hospitable word, even when I saw
The goodliest branch of all my blood lopt from me,
Did I not seal still to thee?

Rut. I am gone.

Guio. And when thou went'st, to Imp thy miserie,
Did I not give thee means? but hark ungratefull,
Was it not thus? to hide thy face and fly me?
To keep thy name for ever from my memory?
Thy cursed blood and kindred? did I not swear then,
If ever, (in this wretched life thou hast left me,
Short and unfortunate,) I saw thee again,
Or came but to the knowledge, where thou wandredst,
To call my vow back, and pursue with vengeance
With all the miseries a Mother suffers?

Rut. I was born to be hang'd, there's no avoiding it.

Guio. And dar'st thou with this impudence appear here? Walk like the winding sheet my Son was put in, Stand with those wounds?

Dua. I am happy now again; Happy the hour I fell, to find a Mother, So pious, good, and excellent in sorrows.

Enter a Servant.

Ser. The Governour's come in.

Guio. O let him enter.

Rut. I have fool'd my self a fair thred of all my fortunes, This strikes me most; not that I fear to perish, But that this unmannerly boldness has brought me to it.

Enter Governour, Clodio, Charino.

Gov. Are these fit preparations for a wedding Lady? I came prepar'd a guest.

Guio. O give me justice; As ever you will leave a vertuous name, Do justice, justice, Sir.

Gove. You need not ask it, I am bound to it.

Guio. Justice upon this man That kill'd my Son.

Gove. Do you confess the act?

Rut. Yes Sir.

Clod. Rutilio?

Char. 'Tis the same.

Clod. How fell he thus? Here will be sorrow for the good *Arnoldo.*

Gove. Take heed Sir what you say.

Rut. I have weigh'd it well,
I am the man, nor is it life I start at;
Only I am unhappy I am poor,
Poor in expence of lives, there I am wretched,
That I have not two lives lent me for his sacrifice;
One for her Son, another for her sorrows.
Excellent Lady, now rejoyce again,
For though I cannot think, y'are pleas'd in blood,
Nor with that greedy thirst pursue your vengeance;
The tenderness, even in those tears denies that;
Yet let the world believe, you lov'd *Duarte;*
The unmatcht courtesies you have done my miseries;
Without this forfeit to the law, would charge me
To tender you this life, and proud 'twould please you.

Guio. Shall I have justice?

Gover. Yes.

Rut. I'le ask it for ye,
I'le follow it my self, against my self.
Sir, 'Tis most fit I dye; dispatch it quickly,
The monstrous burthen of that grief she labours with
Will kill her else, then blood on blood lyes on me;
Had I a thousand lives, I'd give 'em all,
Before I would draw one tear more from that vertue.

Guio. Be not too cruel Sir, and yet his bold sword—
But his life cannot restore that, he's a man too—
Of a fair promise, but alas my Son's dead;
If I have justice, must it kill him?

Gov. Yes.

Guio. If I have not, it kills me, strong and goodly! Why should he perish too?

Gover. It lies in your power, You only may accuse him, or may quit him.

Clod. Be there no other witnesses?

Guio. Not any.
And if I save him, will not the world proclaim,
I have forgot a Son, to save a murderer?
And yet he looks not like one, he looks manly.

Hip. Pity so brave a Gentleman should perish. She cannot be so hard, so cruel hearted.

Guio. Will you pronounce? yet stay a little Sir.

Rut. Rid your self, Lady, of this misery; And let me go, I do but breed more tempests, With which you are already too much shaken.

Guio. Do now, pronounce; I will not hear.

Dua. You shall not, Yet turn and see good Madam.

Gove. Do not wonder.
'Tis he, restor'd again, thank the good Doctor,
Pray do not stand amaz'd, it is *Duarte;*
Is well, is safe again.

Guio. O my sweet Son,
I will not press my wonder now with questions—
Sir, I am sorry for that cruelty,
I urg'd against you.

Rut. Madam, it was but justice.

Dua. 'Tis [t]rue, the Doctor heal'd this body again,
But this man heal'd my soul, made my minde perfect,
The good sharp lessons his sword read to me, sav'd me;
For which, if you lov'd me, dear Mother,
Honour and love this man.

Guio. You sent this letter?

Rut. My boldness makes me blush now.

Guio. I'le wipe off that,
And with this kiss, I take you for my husband,
Your wooing's done Sir; I believe you love me,
And that's the wealth I look for now.

Rut. You have it.

Dua. You have ended my desire to all my wishes.

Gov. Now 'tis a wedding again. And if *Hippolyta* Make good, what with the hazard of her life, She undertook, the evening will set clear

Enter Hippolyta, *leading* Leopold, Arnoldo, Zenocia, *in either hand,* Zabulon, Sulpitia.

After a stormy day.

Char. Here comes the Lady.

Clod. With fair *Zenocia,* Health with life again Restor'd unto her.

Zen. The gift of her goodness.

Rut. Let us embrace, I am of your order too,
And though I once despair'd of women, now
I find they relish much of Scorpions,
For both have stings, and both can hurt, and cure too;
But what have been your fortunes?

Arn. Wee'l defer Our story, and at time more fit, relate it. Now all that reverence vertue, and in that *Zenocias* constancy, and perfect love, Or for her sake *Arnoldo*, join with us In th' honour of this Lady.

Char. She deserves it.

Hip. Hippolytas life shall make that good hereafter,
Nor will I alone better my self but others:
For these whose wants perhaps have made their actions
Not altogether innocent, shall from me
Be so supplied, that need shall not compel them,
To any course of life, but what the law
Shall give allowance to.

Zab. Sulpitia, Your Ladiships creatures.

Rut. Be so, and no more you man-huckster.

Hip. And worthy *Leopold*, you that with such fervour,
So long have sought me, and in that deserv'd me,
Shall now find full reward for all your travels,
Which you have made more dear by patient sufferance.
And though my violent dotage did transport me,
Beyond those bounds, my modesty should have kept in,
Though my desires were loose, from unchast art
Heaven knows I am free.

Leop. The thought of that's dead to me; I gladly take your offer.

Rut. Do so Sir, A piece of crackt gold ever will weigh down Silver that's whole.

Gov. You shall be all my guests, I must not be denyed.

Arn. Come my *Zenocia.*
Our bark at length has found a quiet harbour;
And the unspotted progress of our loves
Ends not alone in safety, but reward,
To instruct others, by our fair example;
That though good purposes are long withstood,
The hand of Heaven still guides such as are good.

[*Ex. omnes.*

* * * * *

The Prologue.

So free this work is, Gentlemen, from offence,
That we are confident, it needs no defence
From us, or from the Poets – we dare look
On any man, that brings his Table-book
To write down, what again he may repeat
At some great Table, to deserve his meat.
Let such come swell'd with malice, to apply
What is mirth here, there for an injurie.
Nor Lord, nor Lady we have tax'd; nor State,
Nor any private person, their poor hate
Will be starved here, for envy shall not finde
One touch that may be wrested to her minde.
And yet despair not, Gentlemen, The play
Is quick and witty; so the Poets say,
And we believe them; the plot neat, and new,
Fashion'd like those, that are approv'd by you.
Only 'twill crave attention, in the most;
Because one point unmarked, the whole is lost.
Hear first then, and judge after, and be free,
And as our cause is, let our censure be.

Epilogue.

Why there should be an Epilogue to a play,
I know no cause: the old and usuall way,
For which they were made, was to entreat the grace
Of such as were spectators in this place,
And time, 'tis to no purpose; for I know
What you resolve already to bestow,
Will not be alter'd, what so e're I say,
In the behalf of us, and of the Play;
Only to quit our doubts, if you think fit,
You may, or cry it up, or silence it.

Another Prologue for the Custom of the Country.

We wish, if it were possible, you knew
  What we would give for this nights look, if new.
It being our ambition to delight
  Our kind spectators with what's good, and right.
Yet so far know, and credit me, 'twas made
  By such, as were held work-men in their Trade,
At a time too, when they as I divine,
  Were truly merrie, and drank lusty wine,
The nectar of the Muses; Some are here
  I dare presume, to whom it did appear
A well-drawn piece, which gave a lawfull birth
  To passionate Scenes mixt with no vulgar mirth.
But unto such to whom 'tis known by fame
  From others, perhaps only by the name,
I am a suitor, that they would prepare
  Sound palats, and then judge their bill of fare.
It were injustice to decry this now
  For being like'd before, you may allow
(Your candor safe) what's taught in the old schools,

All such as liv'd before you, were not fools.

The Epilogue.

I spake much in the Prologue for the Play,
To its desert I hope, yet you might say
Should I change now from that, which then was meant,
Or in a syllable grow less confident,
I were weak-hearted. I am still the same
In my opinion, and forbear to frame
Qualification, or excuse: If you
Concur with me, and hold my judgement true,
Shew it with any sign, and from this place,
Or send me off exploded, or with grace.

THE CUSTOM OF THE COUNTRY.

A = The First Folio.

p. 302, l. 2. A *omits* Lists of Persons Represented in the Play and of principal Actors. l. 49. Second Folio *misprints*] Arnolda.

p. 303, l. 5. A] And that. l. 17. A] a conscience. l. 21. A] Customes. l. 24. A] In the world.

p. 304, l. 25. A] it can. l. 36. A] I A dainty wench. l. 37. A *omits*] I.

p. 305, l. 3. Second Folio *misprints*] yon. l. 11. A] wilde minde. l. 24. A] a heritage.

p. 306, l. 14. A] De'e doubt tis day now. l. 15. A] pulses.

p. 307, l. 32. A] This rogue that breaks.

p. 308, l. 7. A] speake.

p. 311, l. 31. A] alarums.

p. 312, l. 14. A] this marring. l. 15. A] sheckles. ll. 26-28. A adds in the margin] *Boy ready for the songs.*

p. 313, l. 13. A] But such a ransome. ll. 28 and 29. A *adds* marginal stage-direction] *Bowle of wine ready.* l. 31. A] And blushing and unloose.

p. 314, l. 39. A] alarums. ll. 7 and 9. Second Folio] Arn.

p. 316, l. 2. A] Pompean. l. 19. A] Ile ha' your life. l. 20. A prints this line as part of Charino's speech.

p. 317, l. 8. A *omits*] A. l. 23. A *omits*] o're.

p. 319, l. 8. A] Lisborne.

p. 321, l. 21. A] renders. l. 35. A] Lisborne.

p. 322, l. 14. A] aboord. l. 15. A] Yet my disguise. l. 30. A] the contempt.

p. 325, l. 10. A] And he in Lisbon. ll. 22-26. This speech is printed in A as a continuation of Arnoldo's.

p. 326, ll. 18 and 19. A *adds* in the margin] Tapers ready. l. 20. A] so, like a Turke. l. 26. Second Folio *misprints*] Of what. l. 34. Second Folio *misprints*] embace.

p. 327, ll. 2-10. A gives all these lines to Rutilio.

p. 328, ll. 5 and 6. A *adds* in margin] Lights ready. l. 33. A *omits*] Fight. l. 35. A *omits*] Falls. l. 38. Second Folio *misprints*] Governous.

p. 329, l. 4. A *omits*] 1.

p. 331, l. 30. A prints marginal direction] Hold a purse ready.

p. 333, l. 14. In A the words 'my state would rather ask a curse' are printed by mistake between ll. 16 and 17. l. 23. A] sight. l. 30. A] her Chamber.

p. 334. l. 17. A] but to a fortune. l. 21. A] bucket. l. 39. A prints the marginal direction (Musicke) at the end of the following line.

p. 335, l. 1. A *omits*] 1. l. 19. A] strike indeed.

p. 336, l. 1. A] attend her.

p. 341, ll. 14-16. A by mistake gives these lines as a continuation of Sulpicia's speech. l. 33. A] beaten off.

p. 342, l. 23. A] blow that part.

p. 344, l. 12. A] affection.

p. 345, l. 33. A] give that.

p. 346, l. 4. A] may cease.

p. 350, l. 18. A] a larum.

p. 352, l. 5. A] had. l. 13. Second Folio *misprints*] Portual.

p. 353, l. 29. A *omits*] will.

p. 354, l. 25. Second Folio] comanded.

p. 358, l. 31. A] angers.

p. 359, l. 13. Second Folio] you. l. 25 and 26. A transposes these lines. l. 26. A *omits*] not.

p. 361, l. 10. A] hopes. Lords againe. l. 38. A *omits*] and.

p. 365, l. 27. A] it will not hold. l. 33. A] lost me an. l. 34. Second Folio *misprints*] strengthing. l. 39. A] a dores.

p. 367, l. 4. A] adventure. 1. 20. Second Folio *misprints*] unwhosom.

p. 368, l. 38. Second Folio *misprints*] To may you.

p. 369, l. 27. A *omits*] do. l. 28. A] maugre.

p. 371, l. 9. A] sorrowes. l. 27. A *omits*] and.

p. 372, l. 18. A] visitance.

p. 373, l. 3. A] but to read.

p. 375, l. 11. A] Gives.

p. 376, l. 2. A] banding.

p. 379, l. 1. A] a foote. l. 9. A] stick. l. 23. A] welcome home, Gentlemen.

p. 380, l. 36. A] eye.

p. 381, l. 19. Second Folio] If.

p. 383, l. 13. A] Doore in.

p. 384, l. 25. Second Folio *misprints*] rrue.

P. 387, l. 13. A *adds*] For my Soune Clarke.

END OF VOL. I.

CAMBRIDGE: PRINTED BY JOHN CLAY, M.A. AT THE UNIVERSITY PRESS.